I0690605

ROUGH CUT

First Edition

Published by The Nazca Plains Corporation
Las Vegas, Nevada
2010

ISBN: 978-1-935509-95-0

Published by

The Nazca Plains Corporation ®
4640 Paradise Rd, Suite 141
Las Vegas NV 89109-8000

PUBLISHER'S NOTE
Rough Cut is a work of fiction created wholly by *Lew Bull's* imagination.
All characters are fictional and any resemblance to any persons living or
deceased is purely by accident. No portion of this book reflects any real
person or events.

Cover, FleshBlack
Art Director, Blake Stephens

DEDICATION

To Tony for the inspiration and encouragement in writing this novel and to Josh (DK) for stimulating my imagination to create the character Wellington and for the fun I've had developing him.

ROUGH CUT

First Edition

Lew Bull

CONTENTS

1

IN THE BEGINNING

We all have uncles and aunts, cousins and brothers, but some we often tend to forget while others play an important part in our lives. In our family, it was no different, however, there was one small difference, but before I get to telling you about that, I think I need to introduce myself.

My name is Michael Jackson, the only son of Peter and Mary Jackson, who live in Wilton Manors, Fort Lauderdale. As I have already said, we all have cousins and uncles, and I was no different. I had the fortune of having six uncles and five aunts situated in the United Sates, whom I saw on a fairly regular basis when the whole family gathered together like on Thanksgiving or Christmas, and of course the inevitable wedding and rather rare funeral. Somehow our family seemed to live long, so funerals were definitely a rarity. In our family it was not Four Weddings and a Funeral!

You might have noticed that I have said I had six uncles and only five aunts, well that is because I have one uncle who chose to live elsewhere and hasn't married, yet he is by far my most favourite uncle, for obvious reasons as you will find out later. Uncle James, or Uncle Jim, as I call him, is my Dad's brother and lives in London, England, so I don't get to see him very often. However, he does make a point of flying to the

States at least once a year to visit the clan, and when he does the two of us go out and thoroughly enjoy ourselves.

Although there is a bit of an age difference between Uncle Jim and me, me being about to turn twenty-one and him in his mid-forties, when we're together, we have so much fun, that we're like two brothers instead of uncle and nephew and he behaves like a twenty-one-year-old.

Uncle Jim has lived in England for at least fifteen years and has made his money there selling and buying property, so he's established himself in a comfortable apartment in the Chelsea area and has what he calls his 'manservant' to look after him. On the other hand, I've just completed college, not really knowing what I'm going to do with my life. Although I have discussed my future plans with my parents, I still am not sure how to spend the rest of my life. I studied for a degree in sports management and in an e-mail I received from Uncle Jim, he once suggested I should move over to England and take up a career there. It wasn't an idea that I immediately pushed out of my mind, but thought that the sports prospects might be better here in the States.

As a result of my interest in sport, I had developed a pretty trim athletic body and did on occasion go to gym to buff up a bit, but I had never chosen to follow the paths of some of the jocks I knew and become a Mr. Universe look-alike. I would say that my interests were catholic in taste and I enjoyed everything from sport to theatre to music and a few unmentionable things that only my Uncle Jim and I knew about. Living in the Fort Lauderdale area, allowed me to become world-wise to the things around me and this was going to benefit me later in my story.

As my twenty-first birthday neared, my parents had asked if I wanted a party, but I decided I'd rather have the cash that they were planning on spending for a party, as I thought I'd rather go away for a holiday now that my college studies were over. I was glad that they agreed to my suggestion as a week before my birthday, a card arrived from England from Uncle Jim. When I opened it, I read the following:

Happy birthday, kid! Have a wonderful day and if you

don't have a passport, get one immediately.

All the best, Uncle Jim.

I smiled when I read the card's contents. Uncle Jim was the coolest of my uncles. The reason why Uncle Jim was so cool in my opinion was that he was the sort of guy who went out and tried things for fun. He was also very imaginative and I wondered what he had in mind when I received his birthday card. The only way to solve my curiosity was to e-mail him and thank him for the card.

I immediately sent off a message to him.

'*Hi, Uncle Jim thanks so much for the birthday card. I really appreciate it. But what's with the passport business?*'

The reply came back:

'*You're welcome Mike. You know you're my favorite nephew, but I chose not to send you a present this year. I thought you were old enough now to appreciate other things in life and that it was time for you to see the world and how the other half live.*'

Nothing was mentioned regarding the passport.

I replied:

'*Hey, I didn't expect anything, but what do you mean the other half?*'

Immediately the response came back:

'*It's a saying, kid. The reason I asked if you had a passport was because your birthday present is dependent on you having a passport. Have you got one?*'

I replied:

'*Yes, I got one last year when Mum and Dad were planning for us to go to Brazil for a holiday, and then it all fell through.*'

Uncle Jim's answer was as follows:

'*Good, then I want you to make sure that you're available to travel with me.*'

Curiosity was now getting the better of me because Uncle Jim could be very elusive if he wanted to be.

'*Why, where are we going?*' I e-mailed back.

'*Surprise. It's time for you to get to know me better and for you to get a taste of real life,*' came the reply.

'*That sounds interesting, but do I need to know anything specific about this trip?*'

'*Only that you need an open mind and expect fun.*'

This is what I liked about Uncle Jim; he was like an enigma. There were things about him that I didn't know, but then there were things that I was well aware of, like certain aspects of his private life. He had never been shy in explaining that to me and had always been open and honest with me, and that was why I respected and liked him the best.

'*Will you give me some idea as to what clothes I need to take? I mean are we heading for some tropical island, or somewhere where it's freezing cold?*'

'*Your suitcase will be packed for you, my boy. All you need to do is bring your razor, toothbrush and any other toiletries you might need,*' was Uncle Jim's reply.

'*What about accommodation? Where are we staying?*' I asked, hoping to get some hint of information from him.

'*That's all taken care of,*' was his reply. He wasn't going to be sucked into my ploy to get information out of him. '*Oh, and one other thing, please call me Jim and not Uncle. OK?*'

'*If you insist, but aren't you going to tell me anything more?*'

No reply was forthcoming so I assumed that Uncle Jim had decided not to respond to any more of my probing questions.

I mentally agreed to call him Jim as I'd only called him Uncle as a sign of respect, not that I disrespected him by calling him Jim, but we had become very close and were more like close friends than uncle and nephew.

A couple of weeks later, I received another e-mail from Jim telling me to collect my air ticket from the airport and fly to London Heathrow airport and then get myself into the center of London and catch a cab to his address in Chelsea. My flight would be on the Monday to arrive in London the following morning. My parents took me to the Fort Lauderdale airport and I set off on the first leg of a fun-filled holiday with Uncle Jim.

2

UNCLE JIM

I arrived at Heathrow airport in London and caught the underground train into the center of London as Uncle Jim had instructed, then caught a black cab to his address in Chelsea. As we drove through the busy streets of London, a sense of excitement began to fill me and although the driver of the cab had said very little to me on the way, I was now asking questions like what do people do in London for fun, where are all the bars and things like that. You know the typical touristy things.

We stopped outside a very elegant looking building and I emerged from the cab, paid and went up to the front door, where I rang a doorbell.

The door opened and there stood a very large, and I mean large, man dressed in what looked like a long nightgown. He was Black, about six foot six inches, at least, much like those Massai warriors from Kenya, had a bald, shiny head and a serious looking face.

"Yes?" he said in impeccable English with an accent that sounded as though he had a hot potato in his mouth.

"Morning. I'm Michael and I'm looking for Uncle Jim."

He looked at me with disdain, so I repeated my message, realizing I had used Jim instead of James.

"I'm James's nephew," I said, correcting my first mistake by calling my uncle, Jim.

"Ah, yes. Your uncle is expecting you. Please come in."

He stood aside to allow me to enter and then closed the front door behind us.

"And you are...?" I queried.

"I'm Wellington," he said very formally, "but my close friends call me Duke, instead."

"Oh that's interesting. Why Duke?"

"Have you not heard of the famous Duke of Wellington?" asked Wellington, raising an eyebrow as he asked the question.

"Oh yes. I do remember reading something about him in a history class," I answered, without really knowing who the Duke of Wellington actually was.

Just then Uncle Jim appeared.

"Mike, Mike!" He said hugging me to him and kissing me on both cheeks. "It's so good to see you and Happy Birthday for way back when."

I thanked him and returned the hug.

"I see you've already met my manservant Wellington?"

"Yes, he was just telling me about his nickname."

Jim laughed.

"Oh you mean Duke?"

"Yes."

"Wellington does everything for me and really looks after this place. I don't know what I'd do without him," said Jim, smiling up at Wellington.

Wellington returned the smile and took my bag.

"If you would care, Master Michael, I'll show you your room before you settle in," said Wellington, heading up a steep flight of stairs.

I glanced at Jim and he nodded towards Wellington as if to tell me to follow him upstairs.

Wellington hitched up his long nightgown-like garment and for the first time did I notice his open-sandaled feet, which seemed enormous. We moved up to the first floor and along a short corridor and into a pleasant room, decorated in classic style and containing a large double bed that looked as though it was four feet off the ground. It was one of those that you just sink into when you sit on it.

"This will be your room Master Michael. If you wish to get changed you may, then come down and join Master James for tea."

I watched Wellington as he deposited my suitcase and saw how muscular this man looked. I wondered how long Jim had been using Wellington as his 'manservant' as he called him. Wellington had a very open face, large hands, and muscular arms and seemed to more like a giant than a human.

"Uhm, Wellington, please just call me Mike, I'd prefer that, if you don't mind."

Wellington looked somewhat horrified that I should suggest anything less than respectful address and I realized it would probably be very difficult for him to change the way he addressed people; he was like the epitome of the typical British butler.

"Master Michael, so long as you are a guest in this house, I shall be obliged to call you by that name. However, should it happen that we are alone together, out of the confines of this house, I might call you the other name you requested."

I smiled slightly at Wellington's way of expressing his situation.

"Of course, Wellington, but I'd like you to try and call me Mike."

"Certainly sir. Is there anything you would require, Master Michael?"

"No thanks, Wellington."

At which he left and I was able to unpack my suitcase. Once I had finished unpacking, I made my way back downstairs to find Jim. He was in the lounge, waiting for me with the tea already boiled. Uncle Jim can best be described as a man's man. Although he had never gone to a gym, as far as I knew, he had a natural athletic-type physique, was god looking and would attract attention anywhere he went.

"Come Mike and sit down. How was the flight?"

"Nothing exciting, except coming here to see you. But tell me, what have you got planned?"

"Tomorrow Wellington and I will take you shopping and then later this week we're flying to Holland for a few days both for a holiday and for business. Have you ever been there before?"

"No, never. That sounds great, but why do we have to go shopping for clothes? I brought enough things to wear."

"Not for where we're going?" replied Jim, with a twinkle in his eyes.

"I don't think I like the naughty look on that face of yours. I think you're up to mischief."

"When have you ever known me not to be up to something?"

I laughed heartily.

"Never!"

"Exactly, so sit back and enjoy the ride, as they say."

"Tell me, Jim, where did you find Wellington?"

"Do you like him?"

"He looks fascinating."

"Actually, he found me. I was invited out to a party and after leaving it early, I went to a club I sometimes go to and he was there. He was looking for a job at the time and I had nothing for him, so he suggested I employ him as my manservant."

"I love that word, 'manservant'. It's like so old-fashioned."

"Well it just means your male servant, that's all. Nothing out of the ordinary."

"It just seems so English, if you know what I mean. So where does Wellington stay?"

"Here on the premises. He's got a room in the basement."

"Where's he from though?"

"He assures me his ancestors were all from Africa but he was born here in the UK, so he considers himself English, which I suppose he has a right to do, but I like him and we actually get on very well. Before you arrived he asked a number of questions about you."

"Why?"

"I think he gets a little possessive of me sometimes. It's all part of the protective nature he has about him. He believes that because he's my manservant, his loyalty is unflinchingly to me and anyone coming between him and me is seen as a threat. At least that's what I think, but I've never spoken to him about his behavior."

"Is he coming with us to Holland when we go?"

"No, but he will be joining us later."

"Later? Meaning?"

"Later!" replied Jim, without divulging any extra information.

We enjoyed our tea together as Jim enquired about the rest of the family and then after Wellington had given us something to eat, we set off to go shopping.

"Where are we heading, Jim?"

"I want to go to Great Eastern Street first…"

"…why what's there?" I asked.

"I need to stock up on some clothes for you."

"But I told you, Jim, that I had sufficient."

"My boy, don't argue. I'm buying you extra things. You'll see when we get there."

I caught sight of Wellington glancing at me in the driver's rear-view mirror and smile as though he knew something that I didn't.

After driving for some time and maneuvering through the London traffic, we reached and parked outside a store in Great Eastern Street.

Wellington leapt out of the car and opened the passenger door for Jim, who got out and I followed. Wellington locked the car and accompanied us into the shop. We went through the front door and down some stairs which led to a basement. As we reached the basement floor, my eyes popped open wide at the sight of the things hanging there. It was a leather store and all you could smell was the delicious smell of leather. I looked a little surprised at first, but then I knew that Jim enjoyed wearing leather jeans so I thought that he was going to buy another pair.

A thickly-built man with a dark moustache approached Jim and the two greeted each other cordially.

"Hello Frank, how's business doing?" enquired Jim.

"Great, thanks, Jim. Hi there Duke, how are things?"

Wellington and the man called Frank shook hands and seemed to be great friends. I looked at Wellington standing among all the leather and thought his current appearance in his long nightgown attire seemed incongruent to what was in the store.

"Frank, this is my nephew, Mike and I need some clothes for him. Can you help us out?"

Frank greeted me and I reciprocated then he asked what I wanted. I really didn't know what we were doing in the store, so I was dumbstruck by his question.

"I think some jeans and maybe a harness. He's actually got a good body this boy of mine, so a harness will look good on him."

"Do you want chaps?" asked Frank.

"That's a good idea, but then we need the studded jockstrap as well, then," said Jim.

"What size waist are you, Mike?" enquired Frank.

"About a 32 inch waist," I replied.

Frank hurried off to a rack which contained leather jeans, grabbed a pair, and then headed off to pick up a harness, some chaps and a leather jockstrap. Once he had collected everything he brought them back to me.

"If you'd like to go in there and try them on," he said, indicating an area for me to change in, "and if you need a size bigger or smaller, just shout."

I took the garments and did as I was requested. In the meantime, Jim and Wellington busied themselves looking for items they might like.

I stripped and slipped on the metal studded jockstrap. It fitted snugly, encasing my cock and balls snugly, but a little tightly. I immediately took them off and shouted for Frank.

"Could I have one slightly bigger, please?" I asked when he arrived.

"You're obviously quite a big boy then, aren't you?"

I gave an embarrassing giggle and proceeded to try on the jeans, which fitted perfectly. The harness also fitted my chest snugly, so when Frank returned with the new jockstrap, I asked if it should fit as snug as it was.

"Nice body you've got there," he said as he saw me standing in the harness. "Maybe a size bigger to accommodate your buffed chest," he said, heading back to the harness rack.

As the jeans fitted, I took them off and slipped the jockstrap on. This one fitted better as my balls and hefty cock were not scrunched up in the leather material and I felt comfortable. Frank returned with a bigger harness and stood admiring the model.

"You really have got a big package there, Mike, but it looks good in the studded strap. Slip the chaps on and let's have a look."

He helped me on with the chaps and as I felt his hands touching my skin, I began to get an erection. Admittedly it was not only his physical touch that aroused me, but the feel of the leather added to the situation.

"Hmm! That really looks hot," said Frank, standing back and admiring the sight. "And I'm not just talking about the clothes."

Jim and Wellington also came to have a view and both saw my arousal, smiled at the sight, but neither made a comment about my situation.

"We'll take them, Frank. Will you wrap them and we'll be off," said Jim, paying with his credit card.

Back in the car, I asked Jim the significance of us buying leatherwear.

"It's for where we're heading."

"You said Holland, but why the leather?"

You'll see. You're a very curious young man, aren't you, but a very well-endowed one too," said Jim, grinning at me while Wellington smiled from the driver's seat.

"Oh, you mean about the studded jockstrap," I answered, casually.

"Hm! Quite a big boy I would say," continued Jim. "I can see you'll do well on this holiday."

"What are you talking about?"

"Dear boy, just enjoy it and don't be inhibited."

"Inhibited!" I exclaimed. "I don't think I've ever been inhibited."

"No Mike, you haven't. You take after me, thank goodness. I don't know how I would have survived in this family if it weren't for you. You and I are like peas in a pod. Some people think I'm eccentric, but believe me, there isn't an eccentric bone in my body."

"Who says you're eccentric?" I asked, with concern.

"Oh there are people in our family who mutter among themselves and ask why I've never married and when am I going to start settling down and act my age. Really! Age is a state of mind and as long as my mind is active and young, I'll never age. Of course, my body might not be that of a twenty-one-year-old, but my mind certainly is. You see that's also why I like your company. You keep me young. I don't mean to be disrespectful, but some of your cousins are as dull as dishwater. They've got no get-up-and-go about them."

I sat thinking about what Jim had said and realized that he was right. Most of my cousins were boring to me, so I could understand where Jim was coming from. Perhaps if they saw Wellington and Jim together, they even think worse of him, but I think they made an ideal couple.

We headed back into the center of London into Oxford Street and found parking. One of the beauties of London is that you see so many 'odd' people and I mean this with the utmost respect to those people, so seeing Wellington parading down Oxford Street in his 'nightshirt' never turned any eyes. We wandered into a men's store where again Jim knew the sales hand. He seemed to know almost everyone in London, I was thinking.

"I'm looking for underwear, Henry," said Jim, while Wellington stood watch over us.

"For yourself, Jim?"

"No, for Wellington and for my young nephew."

"What size are you, sir?" enquired the sales man of me.

"32 inch waist," I replied.

"And Wellington?"

"34 inch for me please."

Henry, the salesman, led us to a section of the counter where he produced a variety of briefs, jockstraps, G-strings and boxers for our perusal.

"What would you guys like?" asked Jim.

"I prefer briefs or jockstraps," I said, while Wellington said he'd wear anything other than boxers.

I began to visualize, or at least try to, what Wellington would look like wearing a G-string or a jockstrap, and amazingly, I found myself becoming aroused at the picture I had developed in my mind. I tried to imagine what his body looked like under his 'nightdress' and decided that perhaps the jockstrap would enhance his features better.

"Mike," said Jim. "Mike, are you in another world?"

"Oh, I'm sorry, I was miles away," I replied, trying to forget about a half naked Wellington.

I held up a white jockstrap and immediately imagined these against the ebony colored skin of Wellington, and suddenly my cock began to grow at the thought.

"Do you like those?" enquired Jim.

"Actually I thought they might suit Wellington. What do you think Wellington?"

Wellington smiled at my suggestion and then added, "You have very good taste Master Michael, and I would like those."

"You seem to have a good eye," said Jim, taking the white jockstrap from me and passing it to Wellington. "Go and try it on."

Wellington headed in the direction of the change rooms while I continued to scratch through various types of underwear.

"Come, Mike, let's check out Wellington to see if those fit."

We made our way to the change room where Wellington was.

"What are they like, Wellington?" asked Jim, through the closed door.

"Very nice, thank you Master James," answered Wellington, opening the change room door for us to see.

I stared at the ebony torso and huge bulge that was packed into the tight white material.

"That looks enticingly good," said Jim, "don't you agree, Mike?"

I couldn't take my eyes off his package. I could see the long outline of his circumcised cock folded in the material and the hefty balls cupping his cock shaft. If I thought I was well-endowed, then Wellington was a giant. Wellington saw my eyes focusing on his crotch and when Jim wasn't looking, he subtly cupped his balls and gave them a lift, allowing me a better view of the entire package, and then he smiled at me and closed the change room door. By now, my cock was fully erect in my briefs, having enjoyed the sight I had just viewed.

Wellington returned from the change room and smiled at me but never said a word.

"Do you like those, Wellington?" asked Jim.

"Yes, sir, thank you."

"Let's have four pairs of those for Wellington, and what about you Mike?"

"I'll take the same but in my size please Jim. Thanks."

Jim duly paid and the three of us made out way to the car to head home.

My first evening in London was spent in convivial company as Jim entertained me and two of his friends whom he'd invited for dinner. Naturally, Wellington was the ever-present butler who looked after our every need. The friends of Jim were both young men of about thirty and were both in the finance world. They seemed pretty used to Jim's relationship with Wellington as after dinner was completed and the plates had been removed to the kitchen, Wellington was asked if he'd like to join the company with after-dinner drinks. It took a bit of getting used to how one should treat Wellington, either as a manservant or a friend. For me, I saw Wellington as a friend, but I wasn't sure how Jim observed him.

At about eleven in the evening, I decided that I was ready for bed as I'd had a long flight and long day, so I excused myself and left the other four to their drinks.

3

LEATHER PRIDE - DAY ONE

Wednesday arrived and we made our way to the airport, where once we arrived, Wellington dropped us.

"I'll see you on Saturday, Wellington."

"Right Master James. I hope you and Master Michael enjoy yourselves and I'll join you both on Saturday."

We said our goodbyes to Wellington and made our way to the check-in counter of KLM airline.

"We're going to Holland," I said excitedly, almost like a child.

Jim grinned at me and my excitement.

"We're going to Amsterdam for a few days and then who knows," said Jim with a wry smile.

"Why Amsterdam?"

"There's something happening this weekend that I wanted to attend and I thought you might like to join me and so that's going to be your birthday present.

"No chance of any extra clues?" I enquired, but he merely shook his head.

We boarded our flight and headed off to Amsterdam. Throughout the journey I pressed Jim for more information and the only thing that I got was the name of the hotel in Amsterdam, which actually meant nothing to me as I'd never been there before.

On arriving at Schipol Airport, we caught the train into Amsterdam and made our way to the hotel that Jim had booked. As it was situated near the Central Station, we walked along the canals, taking in the sights as we went our way. It was my first visit to Amsterdam, but Jim had been twice before, so he knew his way around. It was with fascination that I surveyed the people and the casual, laid-back way of life they had in Holland. We eventually reached our hotel, The Black Tulip, and booked in.

When we reached our double room, I was somewhat surprised by what I saw. There was a large double bed, which never bothered me, but hanging in one corner of the room was a leather sling, attached to the ceiling by chains. I think Jim saw my reaction and reassured me that I had nothing to worry about.

"If you don't like sleeping with me in the bed, then you'll have to sleep there," he said pointing to the sling.

"Are you serious?" I asked, not quite sure if he was having me on or was being genuine.

"Well, if you want to try it out, we can arrange that," was his reply.

I walked over to the sling and sat on it to see if the chains would hold.

"Lie in it and get the feel," suggested Jim.

I did as he suggested and the sling began to swing with me in it.

"Hey, I reckon I could sleep in this thing," I stated, rocking back and forth.

"Let me show you how to use it, Mike."

Jim crossed over to me and taking my legs, he hoisted them until my feet rested on the chains, thus spreading my legs wide.

"Oh! I get it," I said, blushing at my ignorance.

Jim also smiled at my innocence.

"So if you want to try it out, let me know."

"But tell me, why are we actually here in Amsterdam, Jim?"

"It's the Leather Pride from Thursday to Sunday, so open your suitcase."

I went over to the bed and opened my suitcase. I promptly roared with laughter at what I saw. My suitcase was filled with the leather goods that we had purchased in London, plus a few extra interesting leather items that Jim had bought for me without my knowledge and a few 'normal' shirts. I pulled everything out of the suitcase onto the bed to examine the items.

"You have everything there to last you the week," said Jim, "From jocks to leather jeans, a harness, chaps and boots. Anything else you might need, we'll have to buy here."

I stood and stared at the items, bewildered by the many extra things that Jim had thought of. Amongst the extras was a studded dog collar. I picked it up and looked at Jim. He saw my puzzled look and said, "It's to put around your neck."

I did as he said and looked at myself in the mirror on the bedroom wall.

"And if I want to, I could attach a metal chain to the collar, so you become mine as it were," he added.

I then picked up a small black velvet bag and asked him what it was.

"Condoms, lube, poppers and a cock ring, should you need it."

I opened the bag and sure enough, it was all there.

"You think of everything, don't you?"

"For my favorite nephew, it's always a pleasure."

"So what's on the agenda, Jim?"

"I don't know how tired you might be, but I thought we'd go for a walk so you can get your bearings and then tonight I thought we might go to Stablemaster for a couple of drinks, then the fun starts."

"Sounds fine to me, but I'm entirely in your hands."

Jim and I made our way around the canals and streets of Amsterdam, taking in the people and the various sights. Then we went for a canal cruise under the quaint bridges until we returned to the harbor area, where he took me through the red-light district. I was amazed to see women in windows attracting customers, and then we went into one of the coffee shops, renowned for their products other than coffee.

"Is this legal?" I asked Jim.

"So long as you smoke it in the shop, it is."

The aroma of marijuana filled the air and I was soon feeling light-headed from the intense amount of smoke around us.

"Sorry, Jim, but do you think we can go, I think I'm becoming a little high, sitting here?"

He laughed and agreed to our departure.

"Of course, if you don't fancy the smoking, you could always try some of their magic mushrooms," said Jim, light-heartedly.

"Obviously the Dutch think of everything."

"That's why," he said, "they're so liberated."

After walking for some time, we headed back to our hotel and crashed onto the bed and slept from exhaustion, both from the flight and the walk. When we awoke, it was dark outside so we showered and changed into some clean clothes – naturally it was leather, after all that's all that I had in my suitcase apart from the few 'normal' shirts.

We found ourselves a restaurant to have something to eat and then made our way to the Stablemaster bar, for drinks, or so I thought.

"Why this bar?" I asked Jim.

"I think you'll like it," was his happy reply.

"In what way will I like it?" I queried.

"After eight, the fun starts."

I looked at my watch and saw that the time was nearing nine. We entered the smoke-filled bar and ordered a couple of drinks. I played safe with a beer as I didn't know any Dutch brands of drinks, but I was very pleasantly surprised by the beer that was brought to me. Jim and I sat at the counter chatting to the barman for a while and when Jim saw that our beers were nearly finished he said, "Drink up, Mike."

I gulped down my beer, not knowing why I had to 'drink up'.

"Come on," said Jim, getting up from his bar stool and leading me towards the rear of the bar.

"Where are we going?" I asked.

"To have some fun," was his answer.

We went through a door into a longish passage which led to a vast room which had mattresses scattered around. The lighting was dim, but I could make out groups of men who were lying on the mattresses, enjoying each other's company. I watched as Jim made his way to one of the mattresses on which were five guys, some half-naked while others remained fully clothed. The fully clothed guys were busy sucking on the other guys' cocks and Jim didn't take long to join in. I stood and watched, not sure whether I should join in or not. I'm not a prude nor am I innocent to such things and in fact, one reason why Jim invited me to Amsterdam with him was that he knew I had gay tendencies and would probably appreciate what Amsterdam had to offer.

Jim's mouth found a long, thick uncut cock which he latched onto and began sucking and I saw how he was enjoying himself, so I ventured to his mattress and joined him. My mouth also latched onto the same cock and the two of us slid our tongues and mouths along the young man's shaft, each of us taking a turn to swallow his cock head every now and then and on occasions when our mouths met at the tip of the guy's cock, we would kiss each other.

Soon, I felt someone unzip my leather jeans and felt a hand take hold of my erect cock and then a mouth engulfed it. The feeling of having a warm mouth trapping my cock was exhilarating and I began to thrust upwards into the mouth. Jim broke away and started working on another guy, leaving me to the uncut guy while someone devoured my thick cock. I could feel myself getting closer to shooting, but I wasn't ready to come yet as I was now enjoying the scene, so I also left that mattress and wandered off to another.

The sounds that echoed around the room left nothing to the imagination. Men were grunting, groaning, slurping and coming, but still I held back. I noticed an elderly man had taken Jim's cock into his mouth and was luxuriating on the length that he had acquired to feast on. I knew that Jim was not small in any way and the man realized that he had some prize meat in his mouth. While Jim was lying back enjoying the treatment, he was busy jacking off two guys on either side of him. Soon there were cries as the two guys on either side of Jim let fly their load, some of it landing on Jim's leathers, but this didn't deter Jim. The more they shot, the more he thrust his cock deeper into the elderly man's throat until Jim also cried out and the elderly man swallowed as furiously as he could.

I then saw Jim stand up, zip up his leathers and exit the room, but I was determined to stay a little longer.

I was soon accosted by two guys probably around Jim's age who pulled down my jeans to around my ankles and proceeded to suck my cock and finger my ass. They were working in partnership because the one fingering me was being encouraged by his buddy who was sucking my cock. This went on until I knew I couldn't hold off any longer and with a loud groan, I fired into the warm mouth. The finger up my ass twisted and dug deeper into me, driving me mad with ecstasy as I fired my warm cum.

When I had got my breath back, I too stood up, zipped up and staggered from the room like a dazed, drunken man, to find Jim at the bar counter grinning at me.

"Wow, that was something!"

"You like that?" Jim asked.

What a question! Of course I liked it and I was almost ready to go back for more, except he said I should save myself for later.

"Why, what's happening later?" I asked.

"You'll see," he replied, and ordered me a drink.

"Does this often happen?" I queried, indicating the backroom.

"They have jack-off parties every night, except when they're closed," replied Jim.

At about 01:30 in the morning, Jim and I staggered out of the bar and made our way back to our hotel, arms around each other, more for support than anything else.

Back in the hotel, Jim started to undress me once we had got into our room. He peeled off my shirt and unzipped my jeans, then pushed me onto the bed so that he could pull my jeans off. I lay there in the white jockstrap that Jim had packed into my suitcase and which I had put on that evening.

"You know, kid, you really have got an awesome body," said Jim, almost leering at me hungrily.

"Thanks Jim, but so have you for someone your age."

"Cheeky, hey! Then let someone my age show you a thing or two."

He took me by the hand and pulled me to my feet, led me over to the sling and told me to climb in. I did as he asked and lay there looking up into his handsome face, my cock growing with anticipation in my jockstrap.

"What's this?" asked Jim, grabbing hold of my erection and pulling my engorged cock from the confines of my jockstrap.

"What's it look like," I replied, cheekily. "Do you like it?"

He didn't answer with words, but lowered his mouth to the tip of my cock head and proceeded to lick around the mushroom-shaped head. I groaned with pleasure as he did this and when he felt I was ready for his attack, he sank his mouth over my cock and let it sink deep into his throat. I felt the tightness encircle my shaft and I thought my eyes would roll in my head it felt so good.

Jim's tongue then began an exploratory journey over my heavy balls and between my balls and my pucker. I could feel his tongue rasp near my pucker and immediately my cock throbbed with excitement. I raised my hips to allow Jim easier access to my pucker.

The sharp tip of his tongue punctured the opening and I gasped as he sank his tongue deeper into my opening.

"Oh fuck!" I groaned, and started stroking my cock.

My pre-cum had dribbled from the piss slit and I used this to lubricate my shaft with my hand. Jim continued to explore my chute until he felt that I was ready for him.

He stood up, leant across me and planted a kiss on my lips. His tongue entered my mouth and I tasted my musky essence on his tongue. As out lips locked, so he gripped my nipples and began to twist them between his fingers. My muffled groans were heard and my cock continued to throb. I wanted him inside of me, but he was playing with me, driving me crazy with lust and desire. I eventually broke free from his mouth and gasped as though for air.

"Please fuck me, Jim, please," I gasped in a hoarse whisper.

Jim didn't need to be asked twice. He aimed the broad, bulbous head of his long cock at my opening and slowly began to penetrate me. Although it was painful to begin with, I wanted him so badly, I allowed myself the pain because I knew it would lead to pleasure. He sank deeper into me and as he broke through my sphincter and headed for my prostate, I relaxed. When Jim's cock reached its full depth and was buried to the hilt inside of me, he started a slow, rhythmic thrust and pull action while continuing to massage my nipples.

Jim was always the gentle lover and although he was much bigger than me in cock size, the fact that he made me feel comfortable made all the difference to his love-making. His cock slid effortlessly in and out of my ass, and each time I clamped as tightly as I could onto his shaft, as I didn't want him to pull out. His actions began to speed up a little and I asked if he was getting closer, but he said that he wasn't; it was just that he was enjoying being inside of me.

After some time, he stopped tweaking my nipples and moved to my cock, where he started jacking me off.

"I want to see you shoot, kid," he said, increasing his pace on my cock.

"I wanna come with you Jim," I answered.

"You will. I'm getting close. That fucking ass of yours is so hot I could fuck it all night; and so tight. I wish I'd done this a long time ago," he said pushing in deeper until his balls slapped loudly against my ass cheeks.

"Oh fuck, I'm gonna come, Mike."

"Fuck me harder. Yeah, that's it. Push it in deeper. Oh yes, fuck me!" I cried out as Jim froze and his body went rigid.

A long, drawn out groan left Jim's throat and I felt the first of his load emptying into me. As he fired his warm cum, so he tightened his grip on my cock and stroked it faster, bringing me to my climax. A long spray of white shot from the tip of my cock and I shuddered, my ass clamping tightly onto Jim's shaft, causing him to fire more warmth into me. Between us, we fired load after load until he collapsed exhausted across my body, covering himself in my sticky cum. As our breathing slowly returned to normality, Jim's mouth found mine and he gave me a gentle, yet passionate, lingering kiss.

"Thanks kid, you really are awesome."

"No, it's thanks to you, Jim. Do you know that's the first time anyone's screwed me."

He looked startled.

"You're joking. I thought you'd had it before."

"No. I usually screw the other guys, but it's the first time anyone's fucked me, and you know the best of it all?"

"What?"

"I'm glad it was you first and I really enjoyed it."

"I'm sure you won't forget tonight," said Jim, "because most people remember their first fuck, and I'm glad you enjoyed it."

Jim helped me from the cramped position on the sling and led me to the bathroom where we showered together and then fell into bed and into each other's arms.

The following day was the start of the Leather Pride and Amsterdam had been invaded by leather men from all over the Netherlands and the rest of the world. Jim had explained to me what was expected and what he had arranged for us to do during the next three days – provided I could take the pace!

"Just remember I'm younger than you, Jim, so I should be able to take the pace."

He just laughed at my youthful exuberance, and suggested that I wouldn't be getting too much sleep over the next few days.

"If the first day is anything to go by, bring it on!" I retorted.

He was right!

The first night of the Leather Pride in Amsterdam was a party at a spacious venue, situated in the center of the city, which had two dance floors, a number of chill-out zones, a huge dark room and maze and the inevitable wet room, for those who required it. There was a smorgasbord of at least three hundred men of all shapes and sizes, in a plethora of leather, drinking, talking and meeting men from other countries and cities. Jim and I, dressed in our best leather outfits, mingled among the throngs and soon we found ourselves parted.

As I stood near one of the bar counters, a beer in my hand, a tall dark-haired man, about Jim's age, with a drooping moustache, came up to me.

"You by yourself?" he enquired.

"At the moment, yes, but I did come with a friend."

"Your friend, has he gone away?" asked the stranger.

"Oh he's probably gone to the toilet or checking out the place."

"My name is Heinz," said the burly man. "I'm from Berlin."

"Hi," I shouted above the noise of the music that had suddenly started to blare loudly. "I'm Mike and I'm from the US."

"You want to dance, Mike?"

"Sure," I replied, gulping down the last of my beer and heading to the dance floor with Heinz.

The beat of the music was captivating and soon our bodies were rubbing up against each other; leather against leather, harness against harness. Heinz was physically bigger than me with a broad chest and two extended nipples that looked ripe enough to pluck. He was also slightly taller than me so my face often landed against his chest where I was able to tongue his nipples. Neither of us said a word as it was pointless above the noise of the music, but our bodies spoke immensely. I sensed that he was attracted to me and I admired the attention I was getting every now and then as his hands wandered over my body, but I wasn't sure if getting off on the dance floor was the done thing. As we danced, I caught sight of Jim who gave me a double thumbs up sign and at the same time, I felt Heinz's large hands cup my ass cheeks and squeeze them.

"Nice ass," he shouted above the music.

I smiled back and placed my hands on his leather covered ass. His ass felt large and firm and I wondered what he liked in sex; whether he wanted my ass or I wanted his.

The music came to an abrupt end and we found ourselves in the middle of the dance floor with our hands on each other's ass. However, we were not alone. There were hundreds of others in similar positions, so I didn't feel so bad.

"Can I get you a drink?" I asked.

"Thanks," replied Heinz, wrapping his muscular arm around my shoulder as we headed to the bar counter where Jim stood.

"I'm glad to see you're making friends, Mike," said Jim when we reached him.

"Heinz, this is my friend, Jim. Jim, this is Heinz."

The two men shook hands and I could see from Heinz's expression a little disappointment. I think Jim also saw it because he told Heinz that we were not in a relationship, and then Heinz's face lit up. I ordered drinks for all of us and together we stood at the counter chatting about leather parties and bars in Germany and those in the USA. Of course, I knew nothing of any of this, so Jim took over the conversation. They compared bars and leather festivals, and then they began surveying the other men around the venue, discussing who looked good in their leather and who didn't. For me, the fact that so many men were dressed in leather was in itself a complete turn-on and I was more than happy to stand and watch the others.

"Would you like to dance?" I heard Heinz ask and before I could react, he and Jim were gone onto the dance floor together.

Oh well, I thought, they suited each other, and while they were dancing I thought I'd take a look in the dark room and maze. The dark room was one floor up so I made my way upstairs until I came to a darkened area. Going from the brightness of the dance area to the darkened area, meant my eyes had to adjust, so I stood awhile allowing them to get used to the dim light. I say dim light, as it wasn't completely dark and you could see silhouettes and when you got closer to guys, you could see their features a little better. I wander around the maze cautiously, so I didn't bump into anyone, but it was inevitable that you would touch others.

As I walked slowly along, feeling my way, I felt hands on my chest and then my ass and on occasions, some hands found my crotch. With the constant touching, I had developed an erection and I could feel dampness from where my cock had started to leak pre-cum. Fingers trailed across my chest in search of my nipples and hands delved into the waistband of my leather jeans in search of my hard cock. Some found my meat and soon my zip was undone and a mouth clamped onto my cock, sucking on it furiously. The sound of slurping was distinctly loud and it attracted other men who soon flocked to the sound. Lips locked onto mine and I could feel the tickle of a moustache as the owner's tongue invaded my mouth. I became aware that two mouths were busily exploring my cock while a pair of hands juggled with my balls, clasping them and squeezing until pain shot through my body, causing me to gasp out aloud. I felt as though I was under attack, there seemed to be so many mouths, arms and bodies around me. With all the attention I was receiving, I knew that I'd blow my load very quickly and I was right. I felt my balls rise in their sac, my body tensed and I fired a salvo into whoever's mouth was waiting for my supply. I gasped as each shot left the tip of my cock and mouths were slurping to catch any drop that was being expended. When I had recovered and was able to maneuver my wait out, I zipped up and headed back downstairs where I waited for Jim and Heinz.

They eventually appeared from the dance floor area, but whether they'd been dancing or had gone somewhere else, I didn't know, but they seemed to be getting on very well.

It was in the early hours of the morning that I said to Jim that I was heading back to our hotel as I was ready for bed.

"I'll be along a little later," said Jim, arm around Heinz's shoulder. "Will you find your way back all right?"

"I'm sure I'll be fine," I replied, "and if I get lost I'm sure some nice hunky leather man will take me home to his place," I joked.

I kissed both Jim and Heinz good-night and headed back to the hotel.

I woke some time later to the sound of the chains of the sling in the bedroom clinking. I opened my eyes to see who might be in it, but because the curtains were drawn and the room was extremely dark, I was unable to see, but what happened was like a sensory orgasm.

I lay in bed listening and all I could hear was the gentle movement of the chains as the sling swung back and forth, and added to that was the sound of flesh against flesh. I could hear someone's pelvis thrusting against someone's ass and the constant slapping sound aroused my sleeping cock. With each thrust and slap, this was accompanied by a gasping grunt, much like the sound someone punched in the stomach might make. Someone was being fucked in the sling and I wondered if it was Jim and perhaps Heinz. With each slap of flesh and grunt as the person's cock sank deep into the other man, my cock became harder and harder as I visualized their actions.

"You are so tight," I heard a whisper above the grunts. "I like that," said the first voice I had heard.

It was a German accent, so I knew it was Heinz, but what was more interesting was that it must have been Jim who was lying in the sling with his legs obviously hoisted high above his head.

There was very little dialogue after that and all that emanated from the two men were their grunts, groans and panting until both neared their climax, when they warned each other.

"Heinz, I'm gonna shoot my load," whispered Jim.

"Me too, Jim. Go for it!"

The thrusts, slapping flesh and the rattling of chains became louder and as I cupped my balls with one hand and squeezed my erect cock with the other, the two men shared their juices together.

A long time later, I heard Jim getting out of the sling and felt both men get into the bed alongside of me. I felt a firm ass rub up against my crotch and knew that its owner felt my hard-on because a hand drifted in my direction and latched onto my stiff cock and started stroking it. I immediately draped my arm across the person next to me and let my hand wander down to his crotch. I felt the remnants of a hard-on and a little cum still oozing from the tip, but I knew it must be Heinz because as I slid my hand along his shaft, I could feel his foreskin slide back and forth. He lay facing Jim with his back to me and as his hand stroked my cock I thrust forward as if searching for his asshole, but he never guided my cock in that direction. Instead, he jacked me off until my warm cum shot onto his ass and trickled down his crack, and then he wiped the head of my moist cock across his ass as if making a mark of success on him. After that, we all slept.

When we arose later in the day, I wandered through to the bathroom and saw leather garments strewn around the bedroom floor and there lying gracefully in the sling was a used condom with the remnants of Heinz's juices still in it. I opened the curtains slightly when I returned from the bathroom to allow some light into the room and both Jim and Heinz stirred.

"Morning you two horny guys," I said cheerily when they had opened their eyes. "Enjoy your evening?"

They turned to each other, smiled and kissed.

They obviously had enjoyed themselves.

Heinz showered and dressed, but before leaving, he handed Jim his business card and promised to look out for him at the Friday night's events, and then left. As for Jim and me, we spent most of the day wandering around the city along with hundreds of other leather guys, shopping and doing the usual touristy things.

4

LEATHER PRIDE – DAY TWO

After lunch, Jim said he was going back to the hotel to rest for the evening, but I was determined to see more of Amsterdam and what it had to offer, so we parted ways and I headed down Warmoes Street.

It was a narrow street that had a number of bars and clubs in it as well as a sex shop. Well, at least I thought it was a sex shop until I ventured in and found that it was also a cinema. I decided to pay and go in and see what sort of movies they were showing.

As I ventured in I saw a number of men scattered around the cinema and on a very large screen was a gay sex film. I found a seat and sat down to watch the film. Very soon I was aroused by the visuals in the film and obviously so was the entire audience as men were pairing off and sitting together or heading to somewhere behind the screen.

A man came and sat alongside of me and I glanced in his direction.

"Where are you from?" asked the tall Scandinavian looking man with a mop of blond hair and a blond moustache sitting next to me.

"I'm from the States," I replied, "and you?"

"Denmark. My name's Christian."

"Mine's Mike," I replied. "Are you here for the Leather Pride?"

"Yes, and you?"

I nodded.

After that he never said a word, but his right hand moved slowly onto my left thigh and rested there. With his gentle touch, I could feel my cock throb and grow in size. Then I felt his hand slid over my thigh to my crotch and rest on my swollen cock. He turned and smiled at me.

"You seem a big boy," he said, still smiling.

I had on a pair of denim jeans, which his fingers gently took hold of the zip and drew it down. Once he had unzipped my jeans, his warm hand groped inside my briefs, took hold of my hard cock and extracted it from the confines of my jeans. I watched as he glanced at the size of my cock and then dropped his head onto my lap and started sucking on my cock while I remained watching the film. What with the erotic pictures on the screen and his warm mouth clamped tightly on my cock, there was no way I was going to prolong my desire to offload some juices. I tensed and fired. He swallowed and swallowed, not allowing a drop of cum to escape his lips. When he had drained the last drops from me and I sat exhausted in the seat, he raised his head, smiled at me, licked his lips, put my cock back into my briefs, as best he could, and zipped up my jeans, then he rose and headed to the mysterious area behind the screen where a number of men had disappeared.

I waited some time and noticed that Christian had not reappeared, so I ventured to go behind the screen and see what was going on there. To my surprise, it was a hive of activity. Men were scattered in various corners pleasuring each other and I saw Christian with a middle-aged man, plugged to his cock. I moved closer to him and smiled to him and then knelt next to the middle-aged man. The man's mouth was busily sucking long and deep on Christian's cock so I busied myself, lathering his balls with my tongue in the hopes that I might get to taste his length. I didn't have to wait long because Christian pulled free from the middle-ages man to allow me access to him. His cock slipped easily into my throat and I sucked like a vacuum cleaner until my cheeks were indented I had created such suction. Christian held onto my head and began thrusting in and out of my mouth, while the middle-aged man got up and went off in search of another cock somewhere else. I worshiped the Danish man's long, uncut cock, pulling his foreskin back as far as it would go so that I could lick the tender glans and drive him delirious with ecstasy. With my other hand, I cradled his balls and gently rolled them in the palm of my hand until I felt them begin to rise in readiness of his explosive eruption. Wow, did he erupt! I felt the blast of cum hit the back of my throat and I began to swallow, but his eruptions were so fast and in abundance that I couldn't keep up and soon some of his cum was escaping from the side of my mouth and trickling down my chin. When he was depleted of warm cum, he pulled me to my feet and licked off that which had trickled down my chin.

"Thank you, Mike that was unbelievable. You have such a hot mouth and know how to use it. I'm sure you must be very popular with the guys."

I took that as a compliment and was tempted to say that very few guys had ever had access to my mouth or ass, although I was beginning to think that this holiday with Uncle Jim was certainly part of my growing up experiences.

Christian and I left the cinema together, agreeing to look out for each other that evening at the Friday Party. Having had everything drained from me, I decided to join Jim in having a rest for the night, so I too headed back to our hotel.

That evening, we showered and dressed for our evening out at the same venue as the previous night. However, I had decided to be a little bolder tonight and had pulled on my studded jockstrap, my harness, zipped up my chaps and pulled on my calf-length boots, and to top it all off, I wrapped the dog collar that Jim had given me around my neck.

"Wow, you look as if you're ready for anything and anyone," said Jim, admiring how sexy I looked. "You do realize with your body and dressed like that you could land yourself up in trouble."

"Trouble? Why would I be in trouble?" I asked innocently.

"You look like a walking sex-god and you could easily find yourself being raped by every man in that venue, starting with me."

I laughed heartily at Jim's comment, but when I looked in the mirror, I understood what he meant. Without sounding vain, I really did look sexy and found myself getting a hard-on just looking at myself in my attire.

"That package looks as if it's getting bigger, kid," said Jim, playfully grabbing my crotch. "Hm, it is!"

I blushed but I really felt sexy, what with the aroma of the leather and the soft touch against my skin, I fully understood why guys got turned on by leather. Until you've experienced it, you have no idea what a magnet it is.

"Just in the short time we've been here, I've seen you grow, Mike, and that makes me all the more proud to be your friend and uncle," said

Jim, putting his arms around me and pulling me to him so that my hard, stud-encrusted crotch rubbed against his. "And that feels awesome," he continued, giving my swollen crotch a gentle squeeze.

Jim had decided not to compete against me, so he wore the same leather jeans he had on the night before, but this time he had on a leather waistcoat without a harness and a leather cap placed jauntily on his head.

I looked at Jim and immediately found his whole being sexy. He didn't have to dress like I had to look sexy. He just oozed sex appeal and it made me wonder why he'd never really got someone in his life as a partner. I even contemplated speaking to him about it, but decided to put it on hold for another day.

Once again the evening venue was alive with activity. Guys had made friends and everyone was more convivial than the night before and guys who had, the previous evening, been on their own, now had partners who they'd obviously slept with the night before. The music was no quieter than the previous night, nor was the flow of alcohol any less than before, in fact, things seemed to have gone up a notch, probably in anticipation for Saturday night's events. Jim had told me that on the last night at the Leather Pride, they always chose a Mr. Leather Pride, so I imagined Saturday night would be an evening of sex, debauchery, drunkenness and general fun-making.

We got our drinks once we arrived and Jim soon found Heinz, who had also dressed up for the evening, much like I had. If I really am honest with myself, Jim was right. From the moment we entered the venue, I noticed how men were eyeing my lustfully. It made me feel good about myself, not that I had ever felt otherwise, but to be in such company and be picked out, did wonders for my ego. I could also understand why. Many of the guys were much older than me, had lost their physical attributes, but it still didn't make them appear any less sexy than me. However, I was aware that I had a youthful, manly appearance, with a good body and a heavy package, which made all the difference.

"I told you that you'd be the belle of the ball," said Jim to me as he noticed the men eyeing me. "In fact I think I'm a little jealous. I should hang on to you so they think you belong to me."

I laughed and told him not to be so insecure.

"I am yours, you know that," I said, kissing him passionately on the lips for all to see. "There, does that make you feel better, now?"

He shrugged and told me I was cheeky, but I knew that was what he liked about me, apart from my physical attributes.

Heinz and Jim disappeared onto the dance floor while I remained enjoying my beer and the attention that guys were giving me. A short, chubby guy approached me and asked if I wanted to go to the darkroom but I respectfully declined, saying I was waiting for my friend. He gave a short shrug and minced off. Another two guys, who looked as if they might be in a relationship, because of their physical attraction to each other, came up to me, and asked if I'd like to join them.

"Where?" I asked.

"In the chill-out zone," said the one who sounded Canadian.

"OK," I answered and followed them as they led the way upstairs.

I had been upstairs the night before and knew that the maze was there, but I wasn't aware of a chill-out zone being there as well.

We reached the first floor and ducked down a corridor and entered a dimly lit room with couches and a few tables scattered around. They found a spot and we seated ourselves.

"I'm Chad and this is my partner, Ted, and we're from Canada," said the younger of the two, who looked about mid-thirties or early forty.

"Hi, I'm Mike and I'm from the States."

"We gathered that from the accent," said Ted, who looked about fifty.

"You here for the Pride or are you on holiday as well?" asked Chad, who looked quite becoming in his leather shorts that hugged his tight little ass snugly, a dog collar attached to which was a chain that Ted held firmly, and his harness.

"I don't really know because my uncle brought me here as a birthday present and just told me to be prepared for a holiday."

"That's a very nice uncle you have," said Ted, eyeing me up and down and focusing on my studded jockstrap, "to bring his young, handsome nephew to a leather festival."

"Well, he's my best uncle," I continued, "but are you guys only here for the festival?"

"We flew here primarily for the Pride weekend, but we're thinking of extending our stay and maybe going off to Paris or somewhere else," said Chad.

"Are you in any relationship, Mike?" asked Ted, still staring at my crotch.

I was beginning to become self conscious of his stares and wondered if I should cut short this conversation and say that I was in a relationship and my partner was downstairs. I looked at Chad and thought he was cute, so I relented and continued with the conversation, but changing the focus to them.

"How long have you guys been partners?" I enquired.

"Three years," replied Chad.

"...but we have a very open relationship," added Ted, cutting in rapidly.

"Oh, that's interesting," I replied, not knowing what else I could say.

"Yes," said Chad, continuing, "Ted's very into younger guys; I suppose that's why he chose me."

Now it all made sense. It was probably Ted who was after me and not Chad, but if I were to pick either, I would definitely have chosen Chad.

"Do you know there's a sling area here," remarked Ted.

I actually didn't know that, so I shook my head.

"Come, we'll show you," answered Ted, rising and heading off in another direction.

I glanced at Chad who shrugged his shoulders and also rose to follow.

"Come on Mike."

I joined Chad and we went in the direction that Ted had gone. It didn't take us long to reach the sling area which was vacant.

"Come on Chad let's show Mike a thing or two. Get those shorts off and hop in."

Chad hesitated and then Ted commanded him once more to get his shorts off.

"I told you to get those shorts off, Chad!" he shouted, pulling the chain that was attached to Chad violently.

Chad reluctantly unzipped his leather shorts and stepped out of them. He had no underwear on but I could see that his harness had a cock ring attached to it and a good length of man muscle hung through the ring. Chad slid into the sling and lifted his legs to rest them on the chains, opening up his ass to Ted.

Ted unzipped his leather jeans and pulled out a short yet thick cock, jerked it a little to get it hard, and aimed it at Chad's opening. There was no passion; just blatant sexual lust as he pushed his stubby cock into the young man's ass. The sling swayed to and fro and Chad merely lay there like a robotic creature. I stood and looked on in dismay. Ted pounded away at Chad's ass and every so often Chad glanced in my direction, but he seemed to have a glazed look in his eyes. Almost as if he was drugged. I looked at him, knowing that prior to getting into the sling, he seemed fine, so why the glassy, dead look in his eyes?

I wondered what Chad saw in Ted because it certainly wasn't anything sexual from what I was seeing. It appeared like Ted was master and Chad was merely his slave to do as he wished. I wanted to pull Ted away and take Chad downstairs and away from what he was enduring, but I felt that if I interfered, it might be to my detriment. Admittedly there appeared to be no pain that Chad was enduring, but neither was there emotion. I decided it was their choice to have sex together and not my business to interfere, so I turned and headed back downstairs and went in search of Jim.

Back in the world of unadulterated leather, I found him with Heinz.

"Where have you been?"

"Did you know there was a sling room here, Jim?"

"No. Is that where you've been?"

"It's a long story but to cut it down, yes, but before you get ideas, I was watching."

"That's kinky of you," said Jim, laughing.

"No, I'm serious. There was a couple of Canadians and they took me up there and they got busy, but it was just too ugly to watch."

"Ugly!" exclaimed Heinz. "Sex should not be ugly."

"It wasn't so much the sex; it was how they were doing it that put me off."

"Why what were they doing. This is beginning to sound interesting," remarked Jim.

"The younger of the two was in the sling and he seemed quite a nice guy, but the guy who was fucking him was just using him and although they said they were in a relationship, it looked pretty dull and robotic if you ask me. In fact the younger guy even looked as if he might be in a trance-like state"

"Magic mushrooms perhaps," quipped Heinz.

"No. He was perfectly fine when I was talking to then in the chill-out zone. It was once he got into the sling that his appearance changed."

"Maybe the young guy was the older one's slave and was obliged to do as he was told; to be submissive," suggested Jim.

"I really don't know, but I felt for the young guy. It was as though he was just being used."

"Sometimes this happens," continued Jim.

Just then I noticed Ted and Chad back on the ground floor at the bar, with Ted holding firmly onto the chain that was attached to Chad's studded dog collar.

"That's them over there," I said, without pointing in their direction.

Both Heinz and Jim turned to look but neither knew either of them, so they paid little interest in them, and I noticed that they hadn't bothered to look for me, so I also took little notice of them.

"The young does look quite cute," remarked Jim, "especially in those little leather shorts. Hm! Nice ass too."

As we stood chatting at the bar counter, Christian appeared and came up to me.

"Hi there, Mike, glad to see you here. How are things?"

"Hi Christian. Let me introduce you to some friends of mine. This is Jim, who I'm traveling with and his friend Heinz."

Heinz and Jim looked at me and then at each other.

"My friend?" enquired Jim, with a tone of surprise.

"Yes," I answered. "You are friends aren't you? At least I think you are, after last night."

Both Jim and Heinz saw the funny side to my comment and laughed.

"Hi, there. I'm Christian."

"From?" asked Jim.

"Denmark."

"Ah a strong Viking by the looks of it," replied Jim. "Where do you know Mike from?"

"We met this morning," said Christian.

"Interesting. Where?" asked Jim, who was now enjoying watching me squirm with possible embarrassment.

I tried to get Christian's attention to get him to lie about our meeting, but it was too late.

"Oh we went to the same cinema."

"What did you guys see?"

I didn't have any idea what the film was about apart from it having naked men screwing other naked me.

"I don't remember what it was called," said Christian, in all innocence. "Do you Mike?"

"No. Haven't a clue."

"Why, were you two too busy and weren't watching the film," commented Jim, sarcastically.

I decided it was time for me to defend myself.

"It was a cinema in Warmoes Street," I replied.

Jim grinned at me, knowing I was caught out.

"Oh you mean it's one of those cinemas where they have gay movies all day while you get off with each other?"

"Yes," I exploded. "Yes, that's it. Christian and I met there and I sucked him off while we were supposed to be watching the un-named film."

Now poor Christian had become embarrassed when I'd said that I had sucked him off.

All Christian could say was, "and he was very good too."

Of course that made my night. Someone had made public my prowess in giving blowjobs.

"Tell me, Christian, what's the leather scene like in Denmark?" asked Jim, changing the subject.

"It's good, very good in fact. I'm from Copenhagen and we've got a great place there where we meet. It's well equipped with a bar, a dark room and mazes, and we've got slings and a piss room as well."

"Sounds pretty sophisticated," replied Jim. "And are there many guys who are into leather?"

"Oh yes, but you mustn't think that they're all like Vikings or anything like that," joked Christian.

"Is it open every night?" questioned Jim.

"No, only Fridays and Saturdays, but we make for the rest of the week on those two night," quipped Christian.

Heinz interrupted their conversation and asked Jim if he wanted to dance again, so the two of them headed off to the dance floor.

"What about you, Christian?" I asked. "Wanna dance?"

"Sure."

So we followed Heinz and Jim

While we were dancing, we noticed a bit of a commotion taking place near the entrance to the venue and saw some Dutch police and a few paramedics, but we were aware that nothing untoward was happening inside the venue. When we had finished dancing and the music had temporarily stopped, we made our way back to the bar where Jim questioned one of the barmen as to what was happening.

"There was some trouble outside and someone got beaten up. It looks like there was a fight of some sort. Somebody said something about one of them being a young Canadian."

On hearing the word 'Canadian', my ears pricked up and I started asking questions.

"What exactly happened?"

"I don't really know but I hear the young guy was taken off to hospital. Apparently the other guy was kicking him and beating him as he lay on the road outside."

"I wonder if it's Chad," I mumbled to Jim.

"I wouldn't worry about it. It seems as though the paramedics and the police have everything under control, Mike."

"I'm worried about Chad. Like I said to you, he looked dazed in that sling."

"So what do you want to do about it?" enquired Jim.

"Go and see if he's all right," I answered.

"But we won't know where they've taken him and I'm sure his friend will be with him to look after him."

"Well, I'm going to see what's happening," I continued, marching off in the direction of the police.

When I reached them, I asked the first policeman I encountered where the injured man was and he told me the ambulance had taken him off to hospital and the man involved in the fight was in police custody.

"Where's the man in custody?" I asked.

"He's outside in the police car," replied the efficient policeman.

I headed out to where I could see a number of police cars and went from one to another, looking to see who might be inside one of them, and then I saw him. It was Ted in the police car. I chose not to speak to him to find out what had happened and instead I began to look for a cab to take me to the hospital.

Looking for a cab in Amsterdam at night is like looking for a needle in a haystack – they are very rare and hard to find, but I soon found someone who said he would take me to the hospital. I wasn't sure whether my willing driver offered me the lift because he felt sorry for me or whether it was because of my bulging studded jockstrap and tight-fitting chaps and harness that attracted me to him, but as I was about to get into his car, so Jim came running up to me.

"Where are you going, Mike?"

"This guy's offered to take me there."

So both Jim and I hopped into the man's car. When we got in, I immediately knew why the man had offered me a lift, because the look of disappointment on his face told me he didn't want Jim hanging around. His ulterior motive must have been to take me to the hospital and then perhaps score a night with me in my sexy leather outfit. However, he was good enough to keep his word and took us to the hospital where we found Chad.

He was in casualty having been patched up and was going to be kept overnight just for observations and would be released the following day, if all was well.

"What happened?" I asked when I saw him and also saw how pleased he was to see me.

"It was Ted. He just snapped after you walked away. He said it was all my fault."

"Why your fault?"

"He was expecting me to get you interested so that he could have a scene with you, but I was so tired of being treated the way he does I had had enough and said I wanted nothing more to do with his games."

Seeing Jim standing next to me puzzled Chad.

"Sorry, Chad, this is my friend, Jim. Jim, this is Chad." I said, introducing the two of them.

"Hi, Chad, I'm sorry about what happened to you, but maybe you're better off without him. You don't need this sort of treatment, especially when it's supposed to be a fun night out."

"Sure thing, Jim, but this is always happening. He treats me as his slave both in our lives and when we go out. I fully understand the role-play when we're in a club, but I don't expect it in our daily lives, and that's what's been happening."

"The police have arrested him," I added, "because I saw him in one of their police cars."

"Yes I told the cops when they arrived I was laying a charge of assault against him," replied Chad.

"So what's going to happen to you now?" asked Jim.

"If they let me out tomorrow I'll probably stay to the end of the Leather Pride and then go home – back to Toronto."

"And your partner?" enquired Jim.

"As far as I'm concerned, it's over between us. This has been the final straw for me, so what happens to him, I don't really care anymore."

"Will you be at the final party?" asked Jim.

"Definitely," smiled Chad. "I want to see who wins the Mr. Pride competition."

"We'll keep our eyes open for you," I said, holding Chad's hand and squeezing it. "I've written down our hotel address for you so if you want to call round, please do. So, in the meantime, you rest tonight and we'll see you tomorrow. OK?"

"Thanks for coming to see me, Mike, I really appreciate it because you didn't have to, and I'm really looking forward to tomorrow, now."

We said our goodbyes to Chad and got our 'friend' to take us back to the party.

When we got back, we couldn't find Heinz or Christian and wondered if they'd left to go back to their hotels, which also decided to do, but just as we were leaving Jim spotted them coming downstairs from the darkroom.

"I think they were getting to know each other better," mused Jim, light-heartedly, as he could see the happiness in each man's face.

5

LEATHER PRIDE – THE FINAL DAY

Jim and I woke up early so that we could meet Wellington who was due to arrive today. He was flying in and Jim had arranged to meet him at the Central Station once he had caught the train from the airport. Jim had also arranged with the hotel for a single room for Wellington, so everything was ready for his arrival. I was actually looking forward to seeing him again, and I was sure that Jim also felt the same way.

"Why didn't Wellington come with us when we left?" I asked Jim.

"He said he had some things to sort out and it needed to be done when he was free from his duties."

"Oh so that would have given him time without having to cook and drive for you."

"You make it sound as if I'm totally dependant on Wellington."

"Well, aren't you?" I replied with a smirk on my face.

I knew how close Jim was to Wellington and that he did depend on him.

"Jim, today is the last day of the Leather Pride and Wellington is arriving for one day, so what happens after this? You said you'd tell me later, well now is as good a time as any."

"OK. He's arriving today and then I'm taking you two to Paris for a few days, down to Rome and then on to Germany. That's your birthday present."

"Wow, thanks. It almost sounds like Travels with My Uncle."

Jim laughed heartily and hugged me to him.

"That's why I love you and you're my best nephew. It's that sense of humor that appeals to me, apart from that sexy body you have."

"And the big cock that you love," I quipped.

"Yes, don't forget that."

We went down for breakfast and then made our way through the early morning streets to the Central Station to wait for Wellington.

The train eventually arrived carrying the giant of a man, who stood out above the normally tall Dutch commuters, not only by his dark skin but also by his height. Jim hugged Wellington warmly and then I did likewise, except he lifted me off my feet as he hugged me. Wellington looked very smart in a pair of denim jeans and a T-shirt that looked as though he had poured himself into it; it was so tight fitting across his chest and biceps.

"I am so pleased to see you Master James and you too Master Michael."

"Wellington, you made me a promise back in London, do you remember?" I asked. "You said that when you were out of the house you would call me Mike, do you remember?"

Wellington looked sheepish and embarrassed.

"Yes I do."

"And I'm going to call you Duke from now on until we get back home."

The two of us smiled warmly at each other and shook hands on our agreement.

"It's a deal, Mike, but Master Jim will stay Master Jim."

"Well that's between you two."

"I think you should call me plain Jim, after all, I think we know who's the master in the house," replied Jim.

We walked back to the hotel with Wellington, who had also never visited Amsterdam and booked him into his room.

"I've heard so many stories about Amsterdam," remarked Wellington.

"And I know what you're referring to," replied Jim.

"A man needs good stuff," said Wellington, "so when do we get it?"

"We can go right now, if you're ready," answered Jim.

"Why, where are we going and what does Wellington need to get?" I innocently asked.

"We need a coffee shop," was Jim's brief answer to my question.

Immediately I realized what Wellington was after – his hash or marijuana and maybe a magic mushroom or two, I thought.

Jim led the way and it was like the Pied Piper as Wellington and I followed closely behind. At the first coffee shop, we entered and already there was an aroma to delight Wellington. His face lit up with a broad smile and I could see he was in his own heaven. Jim and I ordered coffee and Wellington ordered an array of varying types of grasses, as I put it.

While Jim and I drank our coffee, Wellington puffed away on his 'cigarette', oblivious of all around him.

"Is there anything else you still need to get before we leave Amsterdam?" asked Jim.

"Maybe a diamond or two or a Van Gogh painting," replied Wellington in his dry humorous way.

Jim took this to mean that Wellington was happy to be on holiday with us and that he was now ready to relax. After finishing our coffee and Wellington his smoke, and having bought stocks of the marijuana that he wanted, we wandered off through the cobbled streets of Amsterdam to show Wellington around. Jim did take us to the Van Gogh Museum where he told Wellington that he was here to show him a bit of artistic culture and not to steal paintings.

When Wellington saw some of the artwork, he commented by saying, "I wouldn't steal that if you offered it to me. I could paint something like that."

"Only in your dreams," remarked Jim, swiftly.

After leaving the Van Gogh Museum, we went to the nearby Rijks Museum for a little more culture. Even I began to wonder at all the culture that Jim was offering us. I was of course, grateful for the opportunity to see other things on our holiday, other than just leather.

We showed Wellington where the venue for the last night party was and then continued to tour the city.

"Where are the men?" queried Wellington, much to my surprise.

I saw another side to the man; one that was completely relaxed and less formal. However, having said that, I never saw him show any disrespect to Jim in the way he addressed my uncle. I was beginning to see a fun side to Wellington and thought that perhaps it was good that he was also going to share the holiday with us.

"I read somewhere about a place here called the 'walletjies'," said Wellington. "Do you know where it is?" he asked.

"It's the red-light district," replied Jim. "What do you want to go there for?"

"I just thought I'd like to take a look there," continued Wellington.

"Oh that's where you took me, wasn't it," I said, butting in.

"Well, if you have already been there, then just tell me how to get there and I'll go on my own," said Wellington.

Jim explained and pointed out the place on the small map that he had in his pocket.

"Oh it's not far from where we're staying," reported Wellington.

"So you shouldn't get lost," said Jim, giving a wry smile to Wellington.

"Are you going back to the hotel?" asked Wellington.

"It's up to Mike if he wants to walk around the city more or go back to the hotel."

"I'd like to visit the Anne Frank house," I said, "especially as I read the diary of hers."

"OK, I'll take you there," offered Jim, "and then we'll meet you back at the hotel, Wellington."

And so it was agreed. Wellington headed off in search of the 'walletjies', for what I didn't know, while Jim and I went off in search of Anne Frank's house.

Jim and I found our way to Prinsengracht and the Westerkerk where we soon found the famous house in which the young girl and her family hid during the Second World War, out of sight of the Nazis, but we were met by a very long queue of young people waiting to gain entrance.

"Do you want to wait and queue or go somewhere else?" asked Jim.

I had been totally absorbed when I had read the book and had traveled thousands of miles to come to Amsterdam, so to miss the opportunity would be a shame, so I decided to join the queue, I think a little to Jim's impatience. He waited along with me for fifteen minutes and then gave up.

"I can't take this any more, Mike, I'm going. You can stay if you wish, and I'll see you back at the hotel."

With that, Jim left and headed back into the center of Amsterdam, leaving me to continue queuing. When I eventually entered the house, I was not disappointed as I could imagine the whole drama that must have unfolded in the confines of the attic area of the house.

Meanwhile in the 'walletjies', Wellington was being seduced by women as he walked past the various windows in which the 'lovely' ladies sat. He was also being accosted by a number of leather men who were also doing what typical tourists do – sightsee. All six foot six inches of Wellington stood out among the throngs of people crisscrossing the canals and as he wandered determinedly up and down the narrow streets he had one thing on his mind. Finally he found a particular doorway. He rang the doorbell and a voice was heard speaking Dutch. Wellington answered in impeccable English and then the door unlocked. He entered and made his way up a narrow flight of stairs, which was a common feature in most Dutch buildings.

Back at the Black Tulip hotel, Jim had showered after his hot, sweaty morning, wrapped a towel around his waist and lay down on the double bed to watch some television. As he lay there, he heard a knock on the bedroom door, so he rose and opened the door.

"Chad, what a surprise. When did they let you out of hospital?"

"This morning."

"Come in, come in and sit down."

Chad came in and sat down on the bed.

"How are you feeling?"

"Much better thanks. It's Jim, isn't it?"

"Yeah, that's it. I'm glad you're better and what's happened about your partner?"

"Once I was discharged from the hospital, I went to the police station and dropped the charges against Ted."

"But why?"

"Jim, I couldn't handle all the trouble of a court case and besides I had really had enough of his domination and so I decided that our relationship was over for good. Please, don't get me wrong; I was in favor of the domination bit when we were role-playing and having sex, but then when we led our normal everyday life, Ted still thought it was part of the sex games, and that wasn't what I wanted."

"I fully understand, Chad. I agree with you about a time to play and a time to be serious. Sometimes I think that some people when they get into the leather world think that they must live the leather life on a daily basis, and it doesn't have to be like that. I thoroughly enjoy my leather experiences and that's usually when I go out to a club or leather bar, but when I'm in the confines of my home back in London and leading an ordinary everyday lifestyle, then the leather and its associated behavior stays in the closet, as it were. By the way, where are you staying?"

"We were booked into a guesthouse near Leidsplein, but with Ted now out of prison, I'm not staying there."

"Can I speak to the manager of this place and ask if he has any rooms left or perhaps you might be willing to share."

"I really don't mind, Jim. I left my luggage at the hotel until I could make alternative arrangements, so I can always go back and get it later."

"Mike and I are sharing this room, but another friend of ours arrived today and he's got a room on his own here, so maybe we can make a plan."

"I'd appreciate that, Jim, but it also depends on the other party if they're willing to let me share their room."

"I'm certain with the plan I have in mind, they won't mind at all."

"What plan do you have?" enquired Chad.

"Let me speak to them first, but either way, you go back to your hotel, collect your luggage and come back. By the time you get back, I'm sure I'll have everything sorted out."

"Thanks Jim. I really do appreciate what you and Mike have done for me."

"Hey, that's what friends are for, aren't they?"

Chad left and Jim returned to lying on his bed and watching the television. A little later, I returned to the hotel, excited at having made it into Anne Frank's house and was eager to tell Jim about it.

"I can't believe how those people squeezed into the space to live under those conditions," I said in wonder.

Jim listened attentively to my story and then he finally interrupted me.

"Mike, Chad's been round."

"Here!" I exclaimed excitedly.

"Yes. They released his partner from prison, on his instructions, and he's going to stay with us here."

"Where? There isn't room for a third, that's why Wellington had to have his own room."

"I have a suggestion for you, Mike. Obviously I'll have to speak to Wellington as well, but I think he'll agree to it. I thought if Wellington moved in with me, then you and Chad could have Wellington's room."

Without thinking, I replied, "Why don't you move in with Wellington and we'll stay here."

"Who's paying for all this?"

"Oops, sorry, I wasn't thinking. Of course I'll move into Wellington's room, but it's a single isn't it?"

"In theory, yes. However their single rooms also have double beds and his particular room also has a sling, should you want to use it," replied Jim, with a wicked glint in his eyes.

Thoughts flashed through my head of Chad and me sharing a room, then I pictured him in his tight little leather shorts and the cock ring and what was in the cock ring and I was sold on the idea.

"Sounds great to me," I replied.

"I thought you'd like the idea. You see I know your tastes in men."

"But what if Wellington doesn't agree to the idea?"

"Trust me, Mike, he will jump at the idea."

When Jim said that, I was more convinced that there was some sort of relationship, other than master and manservant, between Wellington and my uncle. Maybe they had been lovers at one stage or might even still be lovers, I didn't know, but Jim seemed convinced in his own mind that Wellington would buy the idea.

At approximately 4:30 in the afternoon, Wellington arrived back from his visit to the 'walletjies' area.

"Did you find the area easily?" Jim enquired.

"Yes, thanks. It took a bit of getting used to the narrow streets and canals, but eventually I found it."

"And did you get whatever you wanted to do?"

"Yes," replied Wellington, without elaborating.

"Well, I have another question for you. Last night a new friend of Mike's landed up in hospital after being attacked by his partner. Now he's out of hospital and out of his hotel so he came round here and I put it to him that he could stay with us. What I suggested to him and Mike was that you move up into this room and Mike will move into yours, if that arrangement meets with your approval?"

Wellington's face lit up and hastily agreed to the plan.

"If you guys want to leave your clothes where they are, you can always pop in when you need clean clothes, or you can move everything to the other room," suggested Jim.

"Hey, I'm not fussy. All I need is a bed to sleep in and then in the morning I can pester you guys to get my clothes," I answered.

Jim hadn't thought of the 'pestering', which might inconvenience him.

"Maybe it's better if you take your things, I think," he added, once he'd realized that I would be bothering him in the morning.

I packed my things and Wellington went to his room to do likewise, while Jim went to tell the manager of the hotel of our arrangements.

On the dot of 5:00, Chad arrived and came up to Jim's room where we were all congregated. We introduced Chad to Wellington and then I took him off to Wellington's old room.

"Which side of the bed do you prefer?" I asked, being the ever considerate host.

"I'm easy," said Chad.

"I'm not asking you about your sex life," I joked.

He laughed when he realized that I was joking with him.

"You choose," he replied, when he'd stopped laughing.

"I'll take the right, if you like, but if you can't make up your mind you can always sleep in the sling over there."

"I'll stick to the bed, thanks, not that I have anything against slings."

"Are you looking forward to tonight, Chad?"

"Yes and no. Yes, because it will be with you and your friends, but no, in case I bump into Ted."

"Hey, listen, you're coming as our guest and you stick with us. If there's any trouble, we'll get Wellington to sort Ted out for you."

Realizing the size of Wellington made Chad laugh again.

"You know in the short time I've been here, I've laughed more than in the time I spent with Ted."

"Well, I'm glad about that. Now lets' get our things unpacked and sorted out otherwise we won't be going anywhere tonight. By the way, could I ask you a favor?"

"Sure, what?"

"You know what you wore last night, would you wear it again, but without the collar and chain. I really liked those shorts of yours and the harness with the cock ring."

"Only with pleasure, if that's what you'd like."

"Please don't think I'm dominating you or dictating to you like Ted might have done, it's just that I thought you looked so good in them."

"Thanks Mike, I appreciate the compliment, but then I also have a request. Will you wear your studded jockstrap and harness with your chaps?"

"Of course, except I'm going to add something else that Jim gave me."

"What's that?"

"You'll see later. Tell me Chad, how old are you?"

"I'm twenty-eight," he replied.

"Oops, I've done it again."

"Why?"

"I thought you were in your mid-thirties. Sorry."

"Hey, no problem. I'm often mistaken like that, especially by guys who are into the leather scene. And you? I'd say early twenties."

"Exactly twenty-one," I replied.

"Young and virginal," remarked Chad.

"Young maybe, but certainly not virginal, although I shouldn't say that."

"Why not?"

"You won't believe it but I was only recently penetrated for the first time in my life."

"So what! And what was your reaction?"

"I actually enjoyed it."

"Lucky you. The first time I was penetrated was like hell. The guy had this massive dick and I wasn't prepared for it. Although he tried to be gentle with me, it nearly killed me as he slid it in. It took a bit of time for me to get used to his size, but I must also admit that once I got used to him, I thoroughly enjoyed it. So what do you like?"

"Most of the guys I've been with I've either screwed them or we simply had a blowjob, but having now had my virginity broken, I reckon I could classify myself as versatile; and you?"

"I reckon I'm also versatile," said Chad.

"Well, if you're versatile, you won't mind which side of the bed you sleep on."

"Huh!"

"I'm joking."

"I take it that Jim is the uncle you spoke of last night?"

"Yes, and Wellington is what he calls his manservant."

"He looks a big guy."

"Sure is, I mean physically speaking. I've only seen him in a jockstrap and the package looks huge as well, but I've never seen him naked," I said.

"Those sort of guys are always well-hung," remarked Chad, grabbing his crotch as if to demonstrate the area he was talking about."

"Do you mean Black guys?"

"Yes. I've been with a few in my time and never found one who had a small dick. Obviously God blessed them in that area."

"Well the little that I saw, I'd be inclined to agree with you especially concerning Wellington."

"Has your uncle and Wellington been together for long?"

"I don't know much about them other than my uncle said they had met at a club. Now I'm wondering if it wasn't a leather club that they met at."

"What time were you planning on going tonight?" asked Chad.

"I don't know. Why don't you take a shower and I'll nip up to Jim's room and ask him, then I'll shower after you."

I left our room and climbed the stairs to Jim's room on the floor above. I didn't knock and opened the door, but stood my ground as I entered. The view I got was awe-inspiring to say the least. Wellington was standing at the base of the sling with his back to the door. His firm, rounded ass was displayed to me and in the sling lay Jim, his legs hoisted high while Wellington was busy plowing his massive cock into Jim's accommodating ass. With their grunts and groans, they never heard me open the door, so I quietly closed it again and headed back to our room where Chad was busy showering. When he had finished, he came out of the bathroom with a towel around his trim waist.

"So what time are we going?"

I blushed.

"I don't know."

"What do you mean, you don't know? Weren't they there?"

"Oh yes, they were there all right."

"So?"

"When I opened the door, I saw a naked Wellington thrusting his cock long and deep into Jim who was gleefully enjoying every moment while lying in the sling."

"You're joking," gasped Chad, who then burst into laughter. "Are you serious?"

"Absolutely! I could see that firm ass of his tensing and relaxing as he plowed in and out and from the sound effects, both were in their element. I just think it's great that the two of them hit it off so well."

"Maybe my being here was a good thing, because if I hadn't come along, Wellington would have spent his time alone in his room,"

"Maybe we should phone them and ask, except they will still be busy right now. We'll have to wait a while."

"Why don't you shower and then try afterwards," suggested Chad.

I took up his suggestion and went for a shower. When I came out of the bathroom, Chad had on his harness with the cock ring and I stood admiring his athletic body and the heavily hung cock and balls that protruded through the cock ring attached to his harness.

"You know what an awesome sight that is," I said admiringly.

He looked down at his trim, slim body and long, thick cock with its bulbous mushroom-shaped head and then smiled at me.

"If you carry on staring at me like that I'm going to get a hard-on," said Chad, hastily rummaging through his belongings for his shorts to cover himself.

"You're like a painting, so don't cover it up," I pleaded, but he had quickly found the leather shorts and whipped them on.

I saw him draw the zip from between his legs and then I approached for a closer look.

"Hey have those things got a zip that goes right around from back to front?"

Chad demonstrated by unzipping from the front, then the zip went under his balls and between his legs and carried on up the back to almost the waistband.

"Wow! That's handy," I gasped.

"Sure is," laughed Chad, "especially if you're dancing with someone who wants to slip his cock into you. He unzips the back inserts his cock and you dance crotch to ass and no-one knows the difference because the front remains zipped up so they think you are nice and decent."

"Meanwhile you're having you ass plundered in public."

I went into the bathroom with the small bag that Jim had given me in London and took out the cock ring he'd given me. I eased my balls through the ring one at a time and then pushed my cock through the ring as well, then adjusted the package. Immediately I felt myself getting aroused by the fact that something tight was constricting my cock and I liked the feeling. I never showed Chad or told him about the cock ring, but then slipped on my studded jockstrap and harness. I then emerged from the bathroom to oohs and ahs from Chad.

"You said I looked hot, well you look even hotter," said Chad with enthusiasm.

We both finished getting dressed and then I phoned up to Jim's room. A tired sounding Jim answered the phone.

"Sorry to disturb you guys, but Chad and I wanted to know what time we were going to the venue?"

"You're not disturbing us," said Jim, innocently. "Give us about an hour and we'll be ready."

"So long for you two to shower and dress?" I asked, sarcastically, wondering whether they were carrying on their sling encounter on the bed.

Jim didn't know how to respond immediately but said that they had been sleeping and had only just woken up.

Liars, I thought. So we gave them an hour and then went up to their room. Both were immaculately dressed for a leather party. Jim had on his jeans, a harness similar to mine, leather wrist straps and a peak leather cap on his head. Wellington, on the other hand was going minimalistic. He had on a studded jockstrap like mine, knee-length black boots and a harness. Against his dark skin, his attire was stunning to say the least and with his bubble butt protruding from his jockstrap, he looked as though he was ready to be raped by every leather man at the party. Chad's eyes grew wider when he saw Wellington.

"You're right about the package, Mike," he whispered to me. "That's one awesome Black body. I wouldn't mind spending a night with him."

"Nor would I," I whispered back. "Jim's a very lucky man to have that in his bed."

We made our way through the streets. Along with many other half-naked leather men and soon arrived at the venue. Wellington's height, muscular body, beautifully firm ass and well-hung package were the envy of everyone, and Jim could be seen gloating that they were together.

At tonight's party, which was going to be slightly different from the other nights, the organizers were going to choose a Mr. Leather Pride, so we were all looking forward to seeing who was going to be chosen. The usual faces from the last two nights were evident and some new faces also appeared, but somehow there seemed to be a greater sense of excitement tonight. We got ourselves some drinks and then found a spot where we could watch the goings on as well as be near enough to both the dance floor and the bar.

The DJs were pumping out the music, while the constant chatter among friends tried to out drown the music. Those who could find space danced, while others merely indulged in their favorite drink. Jim grabbed Wellington by the hand and led him triumphantly onto the dance floor and immediately other clambered onto the dance floor just to be near Wellington. I could see the proud look on Jim's face and I was pleased for him. Hands were caressing Wellington's bubble-butt while others felt his muscular arms and a few even too a chance by rubbing their hands across his hefty crotch, but all the time, Wellington smiled and danced.

"Come Chad, let's join them," I said leading Chad to the space that Jim and Wellington had found.

"I see you've got yourself some fans, hey Duke!" I shouted above the noise to Wellington.

"Sure thing, Mike," replied Wellington.

For the first time we had called each other by our accepted friendly names. So I felt the barrier was finally down between Wellington and me – we were friends. Chad and danced together for a while and then Jim cut in and we swapped partners so I was dancing with Wellington and Jim with Chad.

"You've got one of the sexiest asses I've ever seen," I shouted into Wellington's ear.

"Yours is not so bad either, Mike, I've been eyeing since the day you arrived," was the response.

I was surprised as I hadn't noticed Wellington taking much interest in my physical being.

"Really?" I asked with surprise.

"It looks neat and tight and that's what I like – a tight fit."

"Well thanks for the compliment, Duke, but I suppose you're not available?" I said with a touch of mocking in my voice.

"You'll never know. If you play your cards right, you might get lucky."

"Like…" I was about to say Jim and then realized that they hadn't known that I'd seen them in their room, so I kept quiet.

"Like what?" enquired Wellington.

I didn't know how to respond so I just smiled and shrugged my shoulders.

Chad, who had been dancing close by with Jim, suddenly danced his way closer to Wellington and me.

"He's here," shouted Chad above the music.

"Where?" I responded, looking around.

"Over by the bar to your right."

I turned to the direction that Chad had said and there stood Ted, glass in hand surveying the dancing.

"Now what?" asked Chad.

"Duke, dance with Chad and when the music stops we're going back to the bar, but stick with him as though you two are together. His partner who beat him up is here."

Wellington moved gracefully from me to Chad while Jim moved over to me. Wellington even took his job a little further by pulling Chad closer to him and placing his arms around Chad's shoulders. It was evident that their crotches were rubbing up together and I could see the delight in Chad's face. Jim and I smiled to one another and when the music stopped, we all headed back top where we'd been standing near the bar.

I knew that Ted saw us, but when he saw the giant Wellington with his arms around Chad, he never ventured closer.

"I think he's afraid of Wellington's size so he's keeping his distance," I suggested.

Chad couldn't bring himself to look in Ted's direction but with three of us around him, I felt he was safe. Throughout the evening, I noticed how Ted tried in vain to get Chad's attention but would come any closer to us. It wasn't until Chad said he needed to go to the toilet that Ted made his move. As Chad went out of the main venue, so Ted followed but I did manage to see his move.

"He's heading after Chad," I shouted to the other two.

Like an army advancing, the three of us followed Chad to the toilet. When we entered the toilet area, we found a number of guys pissing while some were making moves on others and in one corner stood Chad. Ted had cornered him and we could see they were in deep conversation, but Ted's stance worried me; he looked threatening. I went and stood at the urinal and pretended to be having a piss while Wellington moved as close as he could to Chad and Ted without Ted noticing and Jim stood by the doorway to prevent any possible escape route.

A couple of guys were getting deep down each other's throats with their tongues and weren't bothered who watched, while two middle-aged guys were busy jacking off at the urinal and eyeing each other's cocks. I stood there watching the jacking off competition and Ted while Wellington rested his back and butt against a wall, waiting. While he stood there another muscular Black guy moved in on him and groped Wellington's hefty crotch. Duke didn't flinch, but grabbed the Black guy's crotch and squeezed. The man buckled in pain. It was then that Ted turned and saw Wellington still holding the Black guy's crotch with the man whimpering for release. Ted then spotted me and he tried to escape, but Jim was waiting for him. As he reached the exit, Jim blocked his way and by that time, Wellington had released the Black guy and was next to Ted.

"Were you fucking with my man there," He blared at Ted, looking down at the shorter man. "If I ever see you so much as talk to my man there, I'll fuck you up. Understand!"

Wellington stared long and hard at Ted, then crossed over to Chad, put his arm around him and led him out of the toilet while Jim and I stood guard until we thought that it was safe for Ted to go.

"I suggest you go home," said Jim, very politely and calmly. "Chad wants nothing more to do with you or your games, so leave now, or we'll call the police again."

Ted never said a word but scuttled away like a frightened mouse.

"Thanks Wellington," said Chad when they got back to the bar. "Can I buy you a drink as a thank you?"

"Sure, that would be lovely, thanks."

When we reached Chad and Wellington, they were happily chatting to each other as though nothing had happened.

At 11:30 in the evening, the Mr. Leather Pride competition began with eight competitors taking part. The rules were simple: wear leather and obviously be good looking in your leather.

"Why didn't you enter?" I asked Wellington.

"There would be no competition. I must give the others a chance."

All three of us laughed out loud but I had to agree with him, had he entered I was sure that he would have walked away with the title. Not only did he have the looks and the body, but he had a certain charisma about him that made people like him.

Each competitor was brought forward, one at a time and introduced to the audience. Situated among the throngs were five judges who had been chosen from the various sponsors and who sat separately from one another.

First up was number one: Stefan from Germany.

He was a thirty-something bearded man with a broad chest and thick thighs which stretched his leather jeans tightly across his legs, emphasizing them.

Second up was Miguel from Madrid in Spain.

His dark hair and olive skin enhanced his appearance in his leather. In tightly fitting jeans and a well-cut waist coat, he strutted in front of the judges and the crowd. Miguel was clean-shaven but had a one-day's growth appearing on his face. This added to his swarthiness and attraction.

"He's not bad," said Chad to me.

A raucous cheer went up when number three was announced and presented himself to the crowd. Johan from the Netherlands strode forward to wild applause. He must have been well over six foot tall, but not as big as Wellington. He was slightly heavily built and strode with confidence. Dress wise and overall appearance, I still liked the guy from Spain.

Number four: Bruno from Italy was a tall, slim man with blue eyes and a smile to kill for. Being slim, meant that he made his leather clothes fit like a glove and enhance his physical features.

"I don't think he's got any underwear on," whispered Jim into my ear.

I looked and saw how a long appendage stretched down his left thigh. It was emphasized by the tight leather material and I think most of the guys also noticed it because their whistles and shouts were more vocal than those for the Spanish guy. His dark hair was slicked back and his smile was warm and welcoming, but when he turned around for the audience and they saw his firm, round ass encased in the tight leather, they went wild. I then changed my mind and dropped Mr. Spain for Mr. Italy.

Number five came forward, representing France.

He was a short guy by the name of Marcel and had a goatee and a shaven head. Although his leather outfit looked good on him, he didn't match the previous guys in my opinion.

Number six was from Denmark.

As he entered the competition area, Jim and I gaped. It was Christian, our leather Viking. I was pleasantly surprised by his appearance and as we stood admiring him, a voice came from next to us.

"What do you think of him?"

Jim and I turned at the same time and there stood Heinz.

"Why didn't you enter?" asked Jim. "You could have done very well."

"Christian and I spoke about it and we decided that I wouldn't enter and let him have a better chance. Hey, by the way, Jim, here's my business card," he said, taking a card from his pocket and handing it to Jim who immediately put it into his pocket without reading it.

Number seven was from England.

A burly, mustachioed guy with little hair left on his head strode into the judging area. He looked very manly in a rough way, but did nothing for me.

"What do you think, Jim?"

"I reckon I could have done better," he answered, shaking his head in disbelief.

Finally number eight emerged: Ivan from Russia.

Ivan had a small moustache and goatee with a shaven head. He looked good in his leathers which enhanced his physique and it was also apparent that Ivan was also well-hung. There were a number of spectators who liked Ivan's look and probably wouldn't have minded spending a night with 'mother Russia'.

Once each contestant had paraded for the crowd, they were all called on together and then it was possible to draw comparisons.

"Definitely Mr. Italy," said Chad.

"I like Spain," I answered.

"You only like him for the long cock that's hanging in those leathers," quipped Jim.

"So who do you like, Jim?"

"Hm, this is a difficult one. I've got Heinz on my right so I have to say Christian, but if I'm entirely honest, I think Russia might get it."

"What about you, Duke?" I asked.

"It's definitely me," he replied without hesitation. "None of them come close to my appearance."

He was, of course a hundred percent correct, there was no denying it, but unfortunately he hadn't entered.

"Jokes aside, I'd go for ...Germany."

"So we all differ," I said, "but if I had to spend a night with any of them it would be Mr. Italy and it's not because of his cock, either."

The Master of Ceremonies stepped forward after the contestants had finished parading one last time.

"Could I please have the judges' scores," he said, into the microphone.

Each of the five judges came forward and handed in their score cards which the Master of Ceremonies quickly tallied. Once he had checked his scores he went back to his microphone and announced the top three men.

"In third place we have number…eight from Russia."

The well-built Ivan stepped forward, received his runners-up sash, an envelope which probably had a check in it and a bottle of champagne.

"In second place we have… number two from Spain."

Miguel walked proudly forward, hugged his Russian competition and received his prizes.

"And finally, Gentlemen, our winner and Mr. Leather Pride for 2010 is…"

A drum roll sounded followed by a cymbal crash.

"… number four; Bruno from Italy."

The cheers and whistles of approval were loud as the crowd agreed unanimously with the judges' decision and I was excited that I'd chosen the winner. Bruno was given his winner's sash and the other items of prizes then the party started. People were rushing over to the contestants and congratulating them and amidst the confusion Chad and I disappeared upstairs to the chill-out zone.

"You know who I thought was the winner tonight," said Chad, leaning back in a comfy chair.

"Who?" I asked.

"You."

"Why me?"

"Don't you see how great you look in that outfit, Mike? I think that apart from Wellington, you're probably the sexiest man here tonight."

I laughed at Chad's suggestion.

"Are you just flattering me in the hopes of scoring with me?"

"Not at all. When I first saw you it was me who wanted to approach you and talk to you. Ted only saw you as a sex symbol, someone to screw and his idea was for us to have a threesome."

"I've got nothing against threesomes," I responded.

"I'm sure you haven't, but I didn't want Ted to be part of it. You see I was already beginning to realize that I was becoming trapped in the relationship and wanted out."

"But how was the sex when you had it with Ted?"

"In the beginning, it was exciting, but I think it was mainly because it was all new to me. I had never had any experience in the leather scene and he started to teach it all to me. Of course I loved the clothes and still do, but it was when we got to things like S&M and he started hurting me and ignoring my signals, that I began to get concerned. Everything we ever did sexually was so that he could control me. I really was his slave and I don't mean only in sex acts. It eventually transferred into our lives and on some occasions if I looked at another guy or made a comment about one, I would be punished."

"In what way did he punish you?"

"Oh, through his sex. Don't get me wrong, I'm not saying that I disapprove of the odd slap on my ass, I quite like it, or the tit clamp squeezed onto my nipples. It wasn't that. It was when he turned to bondage and constantly tied me up and blindfolded me, then used candle wax to drip on my body or cock or burnt me with the same candle; that's when I realized that things had gone too far. I think the final crunch came when he tried to fist me."

"You mean like a fist fuck?"

"Yeah. I resisted as best I could and the more he tried to force his fist into me, the more I fought."

"Why didn't you just get up and leave him when he tried to do that to you?"

"I couldn't because he'd tied me down so I couldn't get away."

"Chad, I really am horrified to hear these stories, but I don't think all leather scenes are like that."

"You're right, Mike. I know that they're not and that was why I was eager to learn in the beginning."

"For me I think it's more the clothing that turns me on," I said. "If I think about it, I find the touch of leather so erotic that I can get a hard-on just like that," and I snapped my fingers.

"Me too, but I think Ted just went too far."

"I mean if you look at what I'm wearing tonight, I get a hard-on just putting them on. I said to you earlier you would see something that I was going to wear, but I wouldn't tell you what it was. Do you remember?"

"Yeah, sure."

"Well, it's this," I said, standing up and lowering my jockstrap so Chad could see my cock in the cock ring.

"Hey, awesome, you're wearing a cock ring and trust me that cock you've got there is pretty awesome as well."

"Let me tell you, that when I went into the bathroom this evening to put the cock ring on, I gave myself an erection and then when I slipped on the jockstrap and felt the soft leather caressing my cock and balls, I got even harder. This is what it does to me."

"Sounds more like a fetish to me," said Chad, "but I must agree I get the same feelings even though I've been wearing leather for some time now. In fact, I've got a confession to make to you.

"What's that, Chad?"

"I'm sitting here now with a roaring hard-on, just from talking about these things."

"Shall we do something about it then?

"Here?"

"If you want to."

"I'd rather do it with you when we get back to the hotel," suggested Chad.

"Fine by me, shall we go now?"

Chad laughed and kissed my on the cheek.

"Do you think you'll last till we get back to the hotel?" I asked.

"I might have to do something to you before we get there if we don't go now," insisted Chad.

"Come on, then. I'll just tell Jim that we're going home so they don't worry about us."

We made our way downstairs and searched for Jim. I couldn't see him but I saw Wellington.

"Where's Jim, Duke?"

"Would you believe it, with Mr. Italy?"

"You're having me on."

"Not at all, Mike. Take yourself up to the first floor and check out the sling room. That's where I left them."

"You mean you were there too?"

"Somebody had to open up his pretty Italian ass for him."

"And you're good at that, I know."

"How do you know?" queried Wellington."

"Oops, I've been caught out."

"Spill the beans, kid."

"This afternoon I came to find out what time we were going to leave for tonight's party and I automatically opened the bedroom door...

you've got yourself one helluva ass, Duke and I can only imagine how well you use that big dick of yours."

"So you saw me and James?"

"No, let's say I saw how well you plowed into Jim's ass – lucky guy."

"Who's lucky, me or him?"

"He's lucky to have that massive cock plowing his ass, but you because you've got yourself a fine man there and an even finer ass to get into."

Wellington smiled sweetly at me and pulled me to his chest. His lips clamped onto mine and I felt his tongue invade my mouth. I could feel my cock grow instantly hard and press up against his, and then he released his grip and smiled down at me.

"One day little Mike, one day."

"I beg your pardon?"

"One day you'll get to feel what a real man can do for you."

"I think I can feel it already," I said, feeling his growing cock pressed up against my rock hard one.

"You're quite a horny little devil aren't you?" he said, grabbing hold of my erection and squeezing my solid shaft. "Pretty hard too, and big by the feel of it."

"Duke, Chad and I are going back to the hotel, so will you tell Jim, please?"

"Why don't you go and tell him yourself, upstairs and maybe you can use that hard rod of yours."

I looked at Wellington, who looked quite serious about his suggestion and then I looked at Chad.

"Jim's upstairs. Do you want to come up with me, Chad?"

"OK, Mike."

So Chad and I made our way upstairs to the sling room. When we entered there were three other guys watching Jim plugging Mr. Italy's ass. Chad stood to my right and we both stared in awe as Jim rhythmically sent his firm cock deeply in and out of Mr. Italy who lay groaning in the sling. I could feel my cock rising as I watched Jim's actions and at the same time, my right hand slid down over Chad's smooth, leather-covered ass and I felt its firmness. At the same time, I felt Chad's hand rest lightly on my studded jockstrap crotch and run his hand over my erection. Together we stood kike the other three guys as Jim gave a worthy demonstration in pleasing a Mr. Leather Pride.

My fingers rested on Chad's ass and then found the zipper to his shorts. Slowly, and without taking my eyes off Jim at the sling, I unzipped the back of Chad's shorts and let my fingers search for his warm, inviting hole. By this time, my cock was rock hard both from what I was watching and the fact that Chad was feeling me up. Added to this, my cock ring was tightening on my ever growing hard-on and I was becoming desperate to do something with Chad.

"Chad," I whispered. "Will you last till we get back to the hotel or not?"

"I want you to do to me what Jim's doing to him, please Mike."

That was all I wanted to know. I zipped up Chad's shorts, took him by the hand and we almost ran all the way back to the hotel.

Back in the hotel, I ripped off my jockstrap, chaps and boots and stood before Chad naked except for my cock ring which was still holding my cock erect. I helped to take off Chad's shorts and then lay him in the sling with his harness still on, the metal ring firmly wrapped around his equally hard, erect cock.

I lowered my mouth to take in his long cock and lathered it with my saliva, making it slippery for my throat to ingest. I opened my throat and sank down to the base of his cock until I nearly gagged. I heard a long deep sigh escape from Chad.

"Oh fuck, that's awesome, Mike. Oh yes take me, please," he sighed.

I worked on his cock with my mouth for some time and then moved to between his legs, taking his balls into my mouth one at a time and rolling them gently in my mouth.

"Oh fuck, that's good."

Not content, I then headed to his pulsating hole that was just waiting to be invaded. Each time my tongue touched his excited opening, his pucker would clamp shut and his cock would throb. Once I had tasted his opening and lubricated him I moved up to his mouth and inserted my tongue between his waiting lips. We locked together and as I kissed him with passion, so I trailed my finger over his chest in search of his two protruding, ripe nipples. On finding them, each was tweaked gently, sending gentle shockwaves through Chad's body and causing his cock to drip drops of pre-cum.

"Please Mike; you're driving me crazy with desire. I want you inside of me, please."

I liked to hear Chad wanting more. It seemed so different from when I watched Ted fucking him and he seemed lifeless. I didn't want to hurt Chad nor did I wasn't to drive him too far but I was enjoying his taste and II couldn't wait to enter him. When I thought both he and I were ready, I aimed my throbbing cock at his waiting asshole and gently pushed forward until I broke through his tight sphincter. He gasped with wide open eyes, then as I sank deeper into his warmth, his eyes smiled and he looked happy; in fact both of us were happy. When my cock was buried in him to the hilt, I leaned across his body and kissed him. Slowly I started to pull out and I could feel his muscles tighten so that I couldn't escape, but once I pushed back in he relaxed. This continued for a great deal of time and I knew that both of us were floating on air. There was no hurried thrusts, only loving gentle insertions that both enjoyed, and the more I thrust into him, the more he sighs and smiled until he started to jack himself.

"Are you close, Chad?"

"Mm, you're getting me very close, but don't stop."

"I don't want to stop; I want to come with you. Do you want me to come in you?"

"Please. I want to feel your cock throbbing as you fire into me. I want to feel your love passing through me and I want you to stay in me after you've come; that's part of the pleasure you're giving me."

I gave a few quick, deep thrusts and felt Chad tighten his grip on my shaft. He was driving me closer to the edge and he knew it. My speed increased and with it my breathing. Both of us were sighing and moaning more and I could see the perspiration forming on Chad's brow.

"Mike I'm gonna shoot," said Chad, almost crying in ecstasy.

"Shoot baby, shoot! I am coming!"

I felt the first salvo fire into his warm, tight chute and then the floodgates opened. My eyes rolled to the back of my head and I just pushed deeper and deeper. At the same time, Chad let out a cry and I felt a splash as a shot of warm cum shot from his cock and landed on my hand which was busy playing with his balls and then his cum began to pour from the tip of his cock onto his chest and stomach. Both of us shuddered with each eruption until there was nothing more to escape from us. Throughout this, I kept up a gentle thrust stimulating his prostate with each thrust and making him enjoy each moment. Finally when we were satiated and happy, I lay across his sticky stomach and kissed his chest and nipples, licking the occasional drops of his juice as I did so. After some time and my cock had subsided, it slipped from Chad's confines and I gently lifted him from the sling and moved him over to the bed, where we lay for a while warming to each other's love.

That night, I knew what I wanted in life and I hoped that Chad might think the same as I did. That night was not a restful night either, as both of us spent all night exploring each other's body and when the early morning sun began to rise, we were still exploring and searching and touching and kissing and experimenting.

When we did eventually get up, I found my balls and cock sore from the constriction from the cock ring and told Chad I would never be able to have sex again.

He laughed and told me not to be a baby as he'd spent the night still with his harness and cock ring on.

"So what happens now?" asked Chad.

"I truly don't know," I replied. "I like you a great deal, Chad and I'd like to spend more time with you, but I know you've just finished a bad relationship so I don't want to push you into something too soon."

"I'm glad that you said that, Mike, because I really like you too, and I could easily spend more time with you. You're so gentle and caring, which wasn't in my last relationship."

"What were you planning after the Leather Pride, Chad?"

"We were going to spend some time round Europe and then head back to Canada."

"What if I spoke to Jim and asked if you could come with us; would you like that?"

"Do you think you could put up with me?"

"Hey, that's a stupid question. Of course I want you."

Just then there was a knock on the bedroom door.

"Come in," I shouted, and in walked Wellington.

"Well I'm glad to see you two still in bed."

"Why?"

"Well, if you were out of bed it would mean that you didn't enjoy each other's company and couldn't wait to get out. Did you two have fun last night?"

Chad and I smiled to each other and nodded.

"You could say we've been up all night."

"I presume you mean that literally," said Wellington with a smirk on his face.

"Yes, Duke, if you must know, we've been fucking all night."

His smirk changed to a broad smile.

"I'm sure your uncle will be very pleased to hear that," said Wellington as he closed the bedroom door and then reopened it again.

"By the way, where's your studded jockstrap, Mike?"

"Either in the sling or on the floor. Why?"

"I need it," replied Wellington.

"What for?"

"Never you mind," he answered, picked it up from the floor and disappeared from the room.

6

BUSINESS AS USUAL

"Did you get the jockstrap?" asked Jim when Wellington returned to their room.

"Yes Jim and what's more I think there's romance in the air."

"Why, what do you mean Wellington? You mean with Mike?"

"Oh yes. He and Master Chad looked very cozy together."

"Maybe that's a good thing because then Chad could be a distraction for us. I'll suggest that they spend the day together and then we'll have time to do our business. Have you got the velvet bag?"

"It's in the cupboard, James."

"Oh and Wellington, please remember to call me James or Jim, but not Master, even though you think I'm the master, little do most people realize that you're actually the master in our relationship."

Just then there was a knock on their bedroom door.

"Quick, put the things away."

Wellington hid the jockstrap and the small velvet bag and then Jim called out, "Come in."

Chad and I made our way into their room and seated ourselves on their double bed.

"Jim could we have a word with you; it's not private so Duke doesn't have to go," I said getting comfortable on the bed.

"What's the problem, Mike?" asked Jim.

"No problem at all. It's just that Chad and I got chatting last night..."

"...You mean you had time to chat?"

I smiled at his comment.

"In between having sex, yes. Well we had a chat and I wondered if it would be agreeable to you if Chad traveled with us for the rest of our holiday?"

"What do you think, Wellington?" asked Jim, as if seeking top advice.

"Hm, that's a difficult one James. What if Master Michael should meet someone else en route, what will happen to Master Chad?"

"I won't meet anyone like Chad," I responded, to which Jim smiled.

"And what does Chad think?"

"I'd be very happy to stay with Mike, that's if you don't mind."

"I'll tell you what," said Jim, "Wellington and I have to go out as I have a business meeting today..."

"...but it's Sunday, Jim," I exclaimed.

"Every day is business for me," he answered. "So as I was saying, Wellington and I need to meet someone, so why don't you and Chad go off for one of the day tours they offer here. You know like to Volendam or somewhere like that, so you can see the countryside before we leave."

"Would you like that, Chad?" I asked.

"Of course, just to be in your company is great."

"Well, then that's all arranged. You two go off and we'll see you later. Oh, and don't forget we must book out tomorrow, so pack your things tonight," said Jim, giving both Chad and me a kiss on the cheek.

From there, Chad and I went back upstairs to our room and prepared to go and find a bus to take us somewhere – anywhere.

"Right, Wellington, have you got everything?"

"Yes James."

"Wellington, please start calling me James or Jim, for heaven's sake. You do it when we're having sex, so why so formal now?"

"I'm sorry, James, it's just that when Master Michael is around, I like to stay formal; it's part of the cover-up."

Jim laughed heartily.

"I'm sure that Mike knows about us so stop worrying about formality."

Wellington smiled after Jim had said this.

"Why are you smiling?"

"You know when you were in the sling and I was... you know..."

"...fucking the shit out of me," answered Jim.

"Well yes, when I was plowing your ass for you, Mike was standing in the doorway watching us."

"NO!" Was he?"

"He told me, because he said you were a lucky man to have me and that I was also lucky to have you."

"Did he really? Well that puts Mike in a completely different light. Maybe he could be of more use to us than I thought. Don't get me wrong; I'd do anything for that boy because I love him so much and I would never harm him in any way, but I'm glad you told me that. I'm surprised he never joined in."

"Respect, James. I think he's got respect for you and me, and although I know he enjoyed watching us as it, he chose not to be part of our moment together, and I respect him for that too," said Wellington.

Jim hugged the tall ebony man and their lips met, tongues dueling in each other's mouths as they slowly started to get aroused.

Jim finally broke free.

"Hey," he whispered, "if we start something now, we'll never get out to do our business. Keep this for later, my love."

Jim and Wellington made their way through the narrow, and now fairly empty streets towards the 'walletjies' area. Most of the leather men were probably still sleeping and the only people they encountered were the worker on their ways to work. Wellington led the way as he had visited the area earlier but Jim didn't know where they had to go.

Eventually, they came to the wooden door that Wellington had visited. He rang the doorbell and the voice answered. Wellington identified himself and the door was unlocked. Jim and Wellington ascended the steep staircase up to the second floor where they found a door marked 'winkel'. Jim knocked and the door was opened by an elderly man who looked askance at the two men as they stood in the dim corridor.

"Ja?" said the man.

"Hoe gaat het ermee[1]?" said Wellington in his best Dutch.

"Heel goed, dank u,[2]" replied the man, now smiling at recognizing the signaled code between them.

---

1 How are you?

2 Very well, thank you

Jim and Wellington enter the musty room with its single table and four chairs in the middle of the room and its sewing machine situated in one corner around which were scattered bits of material.

"Mr. Schoonraad, this is my friend that I was telling you about," said Wellington, breaking into English. "This is Mr. James."

"How do you do," said the elderly man, shaking Jim's hand.

"I see you have a sign on your door," commented Jim.

"Yes, 'winkel' which is the Dutch for shop."

"I thought so," replied Jim, "but I don't see any goods for sale here."

"Oh but there are," chuckled the man. "Did you bring the item?"

"Yes," answered Wellington, taking the jockstrap out of his pocket and handing it to Mr. Schoonraad."

"Ah, I see what you meant," said the elderly man. "This is not a problem at all. I have two different kinds of studs for you, those that are permanent and the temporary ones, as I call them. I have made two straps for you with elasticized waists so they can fit any size person. Let me fetch them for you."

He moved off through a bamboo slatted curtain into another room while Jim and Wellington were left on their own, not saying a word to each other. Very soon, Mr. Schoonraad reappeared with two black leather jockstraps.

"Here we are," he said, handing them to Wellington.

"These are very well made, Mr. Schoonraad. You are a master craftsman."

"Thank you," he replied, smiling. "I have been making leather items since I was a boy. My father taught me and I carried on the trade ever since. Many of the items you see in the leather shops here in Amsterdam are made by me."

"You're a very talented man," said Jim, who had spoken only now to the elderly man.

"Now, let me show you the studs."

He picked up an old shoe box opened it and rummaged through it, pulling out a handful of different metal studs.

"The best ones are the pyramid shaped ones," said Mr. Schoonraad. "These ones," he said, holding some in his hand, "are solid inside, but these others are hollow inside. Now I can put hollow ones only or mix them; whichever you want."

"Mr. Schoonraad?" asked Jim looking at the studs, "How do we place the items under the solid ones if they are solid?"

"Easy, but the only problem is to get them out afterwards. You will have to rip the lining out to get to them, whereas the hollow ones you can pop them open and re-use them."

"What do you think, Wellington?" asked Jim.

"We'll take one of each, please."

"You are going to wait while I do them?" enquired Mr. Schoonraad.

"Yes please."

"You have the items?" asked the wizened man.

Jim produced his small velvet bag and tipped it out over a cloth Mr. Schoonraad had laid next to his sewing machine. Out of the velvet bag fell twenty small uncut diamonds which Mr. Schoonraad picked up delicately.

"This shouldn't be a problem," he said, admiring the gems.

Jim and Wellington watched with interest as the elderly man took each gemstone and placed in under the base of a stud and watched as the craftsman stitched each stud in place on the leather jockstrap.

"This is probably the most expensive jockstrap I have ever made," remarked Mr. Schoonraad, "and I have made many in my time. You would look good in one," he said, turning to Wellington.

"He does," replied Jim.

"All the Black boys I know here in Amsterdam are well blessed in that area," continued Mr. Schoonraad as he sewed.

"Oh he is too," said Jim, winking at Wellington as he said it.

"You are his lover?" enquired Mr. Schoonraad.

Jim smiled at Wellington.

"Yes and have been for a number of years."

"Hold onto him. With his good looks and beautiful body, not to mention what he might have between his legs, he would be an attraction to many men. I too had a Black lover once, many years ago – lovely man, but he left me for someone else after two years."

A sense of sadness filled his voice as he told them and Jim and Wellington both glanced at each other and smiled.

When Mr. Schoonraad had finished fitting the diamonds in place, he took a piece of black leather and inserted the lining to the pouch. He then handed the article to Wellington.

"You want to try it on?"

Wellington hesitated.

"For an old man," pleaded Mr. Schoonraad.

"Of course," replied Wellington, unzipping his jeans and taking them off. He stood there in his white jockstrap that was bought in London and that too was lowered and taken off. Standing there naked in front of old Mr. Schoonraad with his horse-hung cock dangling well between his thighs, brought a smile to the old man's face.

"That is indeed a wonderful sight," said Mr. Schoonraad in a quavering voice.

Wellington stepped into the new leather jockstrap, cupped his balls and cock and arranged them in the pouch and then posed for Mr. Schoonraad and Jim.

"Oh yes," whimpered the elderly man, "that is truly a sight to behold. Sir, you are indeed a lucky man to have this man as your lover."

"How does it feel, Wellington?" asked Jim admiring Mr. Schoonraad's handiwork.

"Feels fine and fits beautifully. Sure it feels a little heavy because of the diamonds, but that's not a problem."

"Then let me make the other one," said Mr. Schoonraad, fishing out the hollow studs from his shoe box.

In the meantime, Wellington got out of his jockstrap, but to make the old man happier, he remained naked, letting his massive cock hang so that Mr. Schoonraad could see it. The poor man battled to concentrate and constantly licked his lips as he tried to work, but eventually he finished and Wellington tried on the other jockstrap.

"May I show you how this works?" asked Mr. Schoonraad, rising from his seat at the sewing machine.

He knelt in front of Wellington and gently placed his trembling hands on the full pouch.

"What you need to do is pop each of the studs to get them off, then you place your gems in the hollowed out section and then pop them back. It works like a press-stud," he added.

He tried to pop one to demonstrate but his hands were shaking from excitement.

"I'm sorry but I seem to be fumbling," he admitted.

Then he hit on a plan. He slid his hand into the pouch so his fingers touched Wellington's cock and then he popped one of the studs so they could see how it worked.

"There, you see," he proudly said, showing us the hollow inside of the triangular shaped stud.

Again, as he tried to replace the stud, his hand caressed Wellington's cock in the pouch and a broad smile emerged across Mr. Schoonraad's face. He patted Wellington's crotch gently then leaned forward and kissed it and stood up.

"Thank you," he said softly, "that was a very special moment for me," tears welling up in his eyes.

Wellington noticed this and hugged the elderly man close to him.

"You have done a wonderful job, Mr. Schoonraad," said Jim, "now let us pay you for your services, but I'm sure we'll be seeing you again."

Jim opened his wallet and drew out the money that Wellington and Mr. Schoonraad had agreed upon, and then the two men left the building with their two jockstraps.

"Quite an interesting old man," commented Jim as they made their way back to the hotel. "Where did you find out about him?"

"A friend back in London. While you were here in Amsterdam, I was making arrangement from London and then the day I arrived, I went round to see him."

"And?"

"And what?" answered Wellington.

"Well he obviously likes Black men, so I was wondering…"

"Whether I gave him a blowjob or something!"

"Well yes.

"Why, are you getting jealous? Remember what he said; you must hold onto me or you could lose me to other men."

"So did you?"

Wellington laughed aloud.

"Actually, no I didn't give him a blowjob … but…he gave me one."

"Hey you slut!" said Jim, laughing along with Wellington.

The two, when they arrived back at the hotel went up to their room.

"How are we going to do this?" asked Jim.

"If we travel by train, we shouldn't have any problems; it's only if we fly anywhere, because the x-ray might pick them up," suggested Wellington.

"What if we wear the jockstrap? We could say it's part of our underwear and they would see the metal studs and not worry about them?" observed Jim.

"What about Mike? Remember I took his jockstrap to use as a model to show Mr. Schoonraad how we wanted the studs. Maybe Mike could wear it without us telling him of the secret."

"It's an idea, but I wouldn't want o implicate the kid in any way."

"Perhaps not."

"We have to get to Berlin because the buyer will be waiting for the goods and I suppose the quickest way is to fly, but then we'll have to get back here to pick up the second consignment," said Jim.

"I was wondering, why Mike doesn't also wear his jockstrap like me, so that when we go through customs, if the one is triggered off we can explain that we're returning from the Leather Pride weekend," stated Wellington.

"Not a bad idea. We can try it. When the boys return, I'll speak to them, but Mike mustn't get wind of what I do to make my money."

Wellington looked innocently at Jim.

"What do you do to make your money?" he asked sardonically.

Jim shook his head in disbelief.

"Are you having me on or are you being serious?"

"Please, I'm having you on. Of course we don't want the boy involved and I'm not going to say a word."

"Right that's sorted out, now what are we going to do for the rest of the day?" enquired Jim.

"I've got nothing planned so you decide if you want to go out for lunch and rest or do something more exciting."

"Well, I know what the exciting bit would be, but I think I need a rest for a while; your passion exhausts me, babes."

"Oh, so you're saying you can't take the pace."

"No, not at all, it's just I think you've drained ever drop of cum from me and pounded my ass until it's difficult to walk."

"Hell you can talk shit."

"Now that's not the way to speak to your master," replied Jim, trying to take control.

"Honey, you know I'm the master in this relationship. I'm the one who wears the pants here and I'm the one who gets to plough that tight ass of yours, no-one else."

As far as Jim was concerned, what Wellington was saying was true. He had been faithful to his friend as far as not letting anyone get to his ass except Wellington, but he had on occasions ploughed other guys' asses, including Mike's.

"Have we decided what we're going to do, yet?" asked Jim.

"Let's just wander the streets and see what happens," suggested Wellington.

So as nothing else was planned, that's precisely what they did. They wandered down Warmoes Street, passing the cinema where Mike met Christian, and Jim wondered if it was the cinema where Mike had been. Then they continued across until they reached Damrak and walked along the busy street, checking out the locals and tourist alike. The passed Drakes store and Wellington stopped.

"Isn't this the place that's got those glory holes?"

"Quite right. Do you want to go in and see?" asked Jim.

"But do you want to do it?"

"I'll wait here for you. You go but remember with that cock of yours you could be pleasing the entire Dutch nation all day."

Wellington paid and went upstairs to the glory hole area. He wandered around for a while and noticed a couple of other men doing likewise, and then he went into one of the cubicles and sat down to watch the video that was playing in there. Naturally he became aroused watching the video and pulled out his long, thick cock and started stroking it. No sooner had he started when a hand appeared through one of the fairly large holes in the cubicle wall. He stood up and extended his cock through the hole. Immediately a warm mouth clamped on it and started sucking. While he was standing there, another hand came through a hole in the side panel and started to caress his ass, so he pulled his cock back into the cubicle and pushed it through the hole where the hand was caressing him. Again another mouth clamped tightly onto the man muscle. He was enjoying this; then there was a knock at the cubicle door. He opened it. Two guys of about eighteen or nineteen pushed in and grabbed Wellington's cock and both started sucking his massive length. Wellington just stood watching the two young men suck and lick their way to his explosion. His cum flew onto the one's face while the other quickly clamped onto the tip of Wellington's cock to savor some of the giant man's juices. Once they had drained Wellington dry, they stood up smiled at him and disappeared. Before Wellington had a chance to put his cock back into his briefs, another man appeared in the hopes of getting a taste.

"Sorry, buddy," said Wellington, "but the river's run dry."

He zipped up and went back downstairs where Jim was still waiting for him.

"That was quick. Nothing going up there?"

"Oh yes. Two young boys," replied Wellington with a supercilious grin on his face.

"One at a time or both together?" asked Jim

"Together; and one poor soul who came too late."

"Now do you feel better?" enquired Jim.

"Absolutely. Let's go."

They continued their journey down the Damrak until they eventually reached the Central Station.

"Oh we're back here again," said Wellington. "Amsterdam isn't really a big city then, is it?"

"No, it's not, but I like it, and I like the people here."

"Me too. I don't know why you haven't brought me here before. Maybe it was so that I couldn't see the mischief you'd get up to."

"Not at all. I just didn't want you getting hooked on the drug scene, that's all."

Wellington threw a look at Jim that suggested he was talking shit.

"You know I wouldn't. I like my smoke occasionally, but I'm not hooked or anything."

"Maybe, but prevention is better than cure, that's all I say."

"Talking of drugs, aren't you thirsty for some coffee?" asked Wellington.

Jim laughed.

"I get the message; you want a smoke, don't you?"

"Well you have your drug and I'll have mine."

And so they walked until they found a coffee shop to please both their 'drug-related' habits. After they had finished their particular enjoyments, Jim and Wellington crossed a umber of streets until they reached the Vondel Park with its relaxing atmosphere. It was spacious but because it was a Sunday, it was particularly busy with people picnicking, playing games, listening to live music or even, thanks to the way the wind was blowing, smoking up a storm.

"I thought it was illegal to smoke their dope out in public?" asked Wellington.

"It is, and they can only hope they don't get caught."

"I should have brought some from the coffee shop."

"I think you've had enough for today, otherwise I'll have to tie your feet to the ground because you'll be flying so high."

"That's cruel. I'm not that bad."

"No, you're not, Wellington, it's just that you like a lot, and when I say a lot, I'm not restricting it to smoking either."

"You know, for an old man you're very restrictive," quipped Wellington, "but I still love you," he said, kissing Jim on the cheek.

"Thank you and I love you equally as much."

They lay on the green grass and listen to the sounds that surrounded them. It was clear that people were enjoying themselves and the sun was shining bringing warmth to everyone.

As they lay there, Chad and I arrived back from our tour to Volendam.

"It's still early," I said to Chad, "is there anything you'd like to do before we go back to the hotel?"

"Just relax. Maybe find somewhere quiet and romantic to share time with you."

Nearby was a small café and found that there weren't many customers so it was pretty peaceful. We found a table in a corner and ordered something to eat and drink. We sat close to each other I could feel Chad's leg rub against mine and the electric waves it sent through my body was exhilarating.

"Mike, is there anyone in your life at the moment back home?"

"No Chad; never has been. I'm very much single. And you, that is, apart from Ted?"

"I've had relationships with two other guys before I met Ted but they didn't work out. The one was pretty OK, but he was in theatre so he spent more time away traveling with shows so we couldn't really get it together. He was my first. The second guy was an airline pilot; same problem – always away. Then I met Ted and because he had a fixed job, I thought this was the one for me. To begin with it was, but then, as I've already told you, things started to go awry. But what about you? I know you say you've got no-one, but have there been any close encounters that could have gone on to a lasting relationship?"

"You're the first person who's meant something to me, and I don't know why. There was something about you when I first set eyes on you..."

"...you mean love at first sight?"

"Definitely. I just thought you looked a deep sort of person; someone who could enjoy himself, have a caring nature and of course you had all the physical traits I like in a man."

"You mean muscular, handsome, big dick and fucks like a rattle snake!"

"You're obviously not talking about yourself, are you?" I quizzed, laughing as I did so.

"Of course I am, because that's exactly what I want in the man I choose."

"And do I meet those requirements?"

"100% and more, but on a more serious note, what are you doing with yourself back home?"

"I studied sports management and have just finished my studies, so who knows what's going to happen now. My uncle Jim suggested I move to England but I'm undecided. What about you, Chad?"

"As you know I'm based in Toronto and I'm in advertising."

"That's interesting. So I take it you're very creative, then?"

"Well, I like to think I am but you never stop learning, you know."

"Tell me about your family, Chad."

"I've got two brothers who are younger than me and of course my Mum and Dad, and how about yourself?"

"Only child with a mother and father as well as a horny uncle who I adore."

"Do your folks know about you? I mean being gay?" asked Chad.

"I think they do, but we never speak about it. I think the fact that Jim and I are so close, probably gave them the idea that I might be gay, but I really don't know, and it doesn't actually worry me if they do. Does your family know?"

"Yes, I've been very open with them and all my mother wants is for me to settle down and find a 'nice young man' as she puts it."

"Am I a 'nice young man'?" I asked.

"I think she'd like you a lot and so would my Dad…"

"Maybe I'll forego the son and marry the father instead," I joked.

"I'm serious, I really think he'd like you; sporty and all that."

"Are your brothers as good looking as you?"

"I should say no so that you don't go for one of them, but I'd be lying. I think they're stunners and I'm afraid you might like them more than me if you met them, so I'd better keep you well away from them."

"Now you're getting me interested. Are they much younger than you?"

"I'm not saying anything more about them otherwise I'll definitely lose you to them."

"Ah, come on, just play nicely with me."

"Greg is twenty-four and Marc is twenty, so now you know."

"Hm, interesting ages."

"Meaning?"

"They could follow in big brother's footsteps."

"I doubt it. Greg's got himself a girlfriend and fucks the hell out of her, or so he says, but you know how boys exaggerate sometimes, but of the two, Marc is the silent type."

"Well, there you go; Marc's the young one to be trained to follow big brother."

"You know that mind of yours is warped. But tell me where do you think Jim will be going after you leave Amsterdam?"

"I really have no idea. I've heard places named but nothing has been said top me. Maybe when we get back to the hotel I'll ask and then we'll know for sure where we're heading."

"I hope it's somewhere romantic," said Chad, his leg rubbing up against mine.

"You're quite a romantic at heart aren't you?"

"I suppose I am. It's just that I like romancing my partners but of course, some of them don't like it. How about you?" asked Chad.

"If you mean would I go on a candle-lit cruise round the canals of Amsterdam, for example, I'd say let's go."

"Would you really?"

"Of course. Shall we do it tonight?"

"Oh, yes, please let's do it Mike."

"Is that a date you're asking me on?"

"If you want to put it that way; yes. And do you accept?"

"Only with the greatest of pleasure."

We finished our drinks and snacks that we'd ordered, paid and headed back in the direction of the hotel. As we neared the canals we could see the glass-topped canal boats waiting for their tourists to board and Chad pointed to one and asked, "Is that the one we're going on?"

"If you'd like, yes," replied.

Back at the hotel, we enquired if Jim and Wellington were back and the receptionist said they were, so Chad and I went directly to their room. We knocked, for safety sake and heard Jim's voice call us in.

"Hi guys, how was your tour?"

"Great, thanks Jim."

"And did you enjoy yourselves?"

"Absolutely," said Chad. "We saw people in traditional Dutch clothes and ate 'poffertjies' which were tiny pancakes and were delicious…"

".. And we saw a windmill," I interrupted, excitedly, "and tonight I'm taking Chad for a romantic canal cruise."

Wellington and Jim smiled at my suggestion but didn't make fun of our idea.

"Oh we thought we'd just go to bed," said Jim, with a touch of boredom in his voice.

"Don't make it sound so tiresome, Jim, I know how wild you and Duke can get when you go to bed," I retorted.

"Don't forget to pack tonight because we're leaving tomorrow," said Jim, probably broaching the topic of the jockstrap.

"Where are we going, Jim?" I asked.

"I thought of Paris, but I have to go to Berlin on business, so we're flying out tomorrow morning. I've booked for four, so Chad that means you're coming to Berlin as well."

"Thanks Jim, I really appreciate that," replied Chad, hugging me as he thanked Jim.

"So why don't you go upstairs and start packing your bags."

As we were about to leave, Jim called me back.

"Shut the door, Mike. Tomorrow when we go to the airport try to carry as little luggage as possible. Rather put it in the hold of the plane."

"I actually have very little, Jim."

"What Wellington and I thought, because leather is quite a heavy material, it might be best to wear as much of your leather as possible to lighten your suitcase, so I'd suggest put on your leather jeans and jockstrap, for example."

"Wellington took mine but hasn't given it back."

"Sorry, Mike, here it is," said Wellington handing me the studded jockstrap.

"Thanks Duke," I said, taking the jockstrap and heading up to our room.

When I arrived, Chad was busy packing his bag.

"Jim says we should wear as much of our leather so that our bags become lighter," I relayed to Chad.

"So what are you gonna wear?"

"I thought my jockstrap, leather jeans and boots. The harness shouldn't take up too much space and the collar and cock ring are nothing weight wise."

"I'll probably do the same then," said Chad, unpacking some of his leatherwear.

We laid out our clothes for the airport, packed the others and kept what we wanted for the evening out.

"Was Jim serious about them going to bed?"

"I wouldn't know with them, but I didn't want to invite them along as I wanted to spend time with you."

"Thanks Mike, I appreciate that," said Chad putting his arms around my neck and kissing me passionately.

"You're such a beautiful man, you know that?" he said when our lips parted.

Our cruise on the canals was probably one of the highlights of my trip to Amsterdam. There were romantic candles in the glass-topped boat and as we sailed the lights flickered from the breeze. Whenever we passed a bridge, the moment became more romantic as each bridge was lit up with lights. We were offered chesses and wine to add to the occasion and the only sounds were the rustling of the waves as the boat made its way along the various canals. Chad sat next to me, his hand resting on my thigh and both of us were in a heaven-like state. It was only once we reached our final destination that we were brought back to reality and realized what a stunning evening we had enjoyed. Chad, being the romantic that he is, kissed me excitedly once we were on land and thanked me profusely for the evening. I think this man is truly in love with me.

7

PROBLEMS IN BERLIN

Bright and early the following morning, we were all up and getting ready to depart to Berlin. Jim picked up his leather jeans to put on and as he did so the business card Heinz had given to him, fell from one of the pockets. Jim bent to pick it up and read the writing on it for the first time.

"Oh God!" he exclaimed.

"What's the matter?" enquired Wellington as he finished dressing.

"I've just read Heinz's business card. Do you know what he does?"

"No, so tell me."

"Criminal Investigation Department. Heinz Schmidt. I don't know if that's a good thing or not. At least we know one policeman who's ready to drop his leathers if he likes the other guy, but I hope we don't bump into him searching us at the Berlin airport."

"I doubt it," stated Wellington, not taking it too seriously. But does he live in Berlin?"

"That's what it says here on the card."

"Oh well, maybe it might be a good thing if he is at the airport because then you or I could make a pass at him and hope to get through that way."

"Just be positive, Wellington. We are going to get through and we are going to get rid of the diamonds and we are going to get a substantial amount of money," repeated Jim.

We walked from the hotel to the Central Station where we caught the train to Schipol Airport. Once at the airport, we found the check-in counter and booked in our luggage, got our boarding passes and went to passport control; but before we reached that area, we were obliged to go through the hand-luggage and body search. Jim went through without any trouble and was followed by Wellington. As he passed through the body search, the buzzer went off.

"Could you go back again, sir," said the officious guard.

Wellington did so and again the alarm went off. The guard took him to one side and started feeling to see of he had any hidden weapons or such things on his body. In the meantime, I went through. The alarms sounded and I was requested to go through again. On my second passing, the alarm sounded again, so I was pulled to one side and felt. Chad, in the meantime had made it through with Jim.

After the hand search, both Wellington and I were made to go through again. Once more alarm bells rang for both of us.

"Could you please come with us," said the guard, who then led Wellington and me off to a room.

"Would you mind stripping please?" requested the guard.

Wellington stripped first and when the guard saw him wearing a studded jockstrap he smiled.

"It is possibly that," he said pointing to the metal studs. "But please remove that too."

Wellington slid his jockstrap off and when the guard saw the size of his flaccid cock, his eyes bulged and his jaw dropped open.

"Thank you sir, I'm sure that will be fine, thank you."

I decided to speak up then.

"I think I'm in the same situation as him, sir. You see I also have a studded jockstrap on which probably set off the alarm."

"Please drop your jeans."

I did as was requested and the guard saw I wasn't lying, but not to be left without a look, he also asked me to take mine off. I did as was asked and his smile told me either he liked what he saw or he thought I was a midget in comparison to Wellington's massive length. We were taken back to the control area and allowed to pass, much to Jim's delight.

"I was getting worried there," he whispered to Wellington.

"Nothing to worry about, they bought it and both of us were stripped but they found nothing."

We boarded our plane and were soon flying on our way to Berlin.

We landed at Tegel Airport which was only five miles from the center of Berlin. We disembarked and went from passport control to collect our luggage. We waited a while for our bags to arrive, but once they did we made our way through customs. As we had nothing to declare, we went through the green area, but as Wellington approached, a burly German guard stepped forward and called him to one side. Jim hesitated to wait for Wellington and told both Chad and me to carry on and go through.

"Where have you come from?" asked the burly guard, who himself would have looked good in leather.

"From Amsterdam," said Wellington. "We went there for the Leather Pride," he added.

"Please open your luggage."

Wellington opened his suitcase and an array of leather items met the guard's eyes. The guard, who had on a name badge marked Helmut, carefully picked up each item, feeling its soft touch, and then he found the extra studded jockstrap and looked carefully at it. He found some condoms, lube and two cock rings, again which he casually picked up and looked at their size. He held one up to Wellington.

"Yours?" he asked.

"Yes, sir," replied Wellington.

The guard turned the ring around in his hand and then casually said, "Big!"

He continued scratching through Wellington's suitcase and then found a pair of leather boots. He slid his hand down the sides of one and then inserted his hand into the boot. As he withdrew his hand, he looked up at Wellington and smiled. In his hand was a sachet filled with marijuana.

"You coming from Amsterdam, ja? This is not Amsterdam. You better come with me."

"Where are you taking him?" interrupted Jim. "We're traveling together so I need to know where he'll be."

"We need to ask more questions," said the guard with a touch of venom in his voice. "Please close your suitcase and come with me."

Wellington and the burly guard went into a room which was closed to the public.

"What must I do?" shouted Jim as Wellington disappeared into the room.

The obvious thing to do, if Wellington was going to be arrested was call Heinz, he thought.

In the room another guard joined the burly one, except the second one looked like someone who'd been on a strict diet all his life. He wasn't thin; he was skinny. They emptied Wellington's suitcase onto a table and began to inspect each piece of clothing, inside and out. When they had finished, another younger man appeared and whispered something to the burly guard, who immediately glanced at Wellington.

"Strip!" he commanded.

The skinny guard was taken by surprise by his colleague's command. Wellington began what can only be described as a seductive strip act. First he removed his shirt to reveal his dark, muscular chest with the over-ripe nipples. Then he unzipped his leather jeans and seductively wriggled out of them, and then he teased them with his studded jockstrap. His cock flopped out of the jockstrap and all the guards stood in awe. Wellington, not to be outdone hadn't finished his act. He placed a hand under his heavy balls and scooped them up showing his audience how big they were, and the as a finale, he stroked his massive cock as though to wake it up from its slumber. When he let go of it, it must have grown an inch or two more. He stood there buck naked, his ebony skin shining in the light of the room.

Although the guards were clearly impressed by what they saw, they still had a job of work to do. While the burly guard began a physical body search the skinny one inspected the jockstrap. Throughout this Wellington eyed the skinny one to see if he found the uncut diamonds, which as far as he was concerned was more of a crime than the marijuana.

The burly guard's hands felt inside Wellington's thigh and then his balls, then his hands moved to Wellington's ass and he felt as the burly man's fingers traced along his ass crack and then a digit entered Wellington's ass.

"Ooh, that feels good," said Wellington, whose cock was beginning to grow in size from the guard's touches.

Two fingers were inserted and they went in deeper.

Wellington wriggled his ass slightly to allow the guard's finger to go deeper. By now Wellington's cock was almost vertically erect, but the guard was not about to stop. A third digit was inserted and this spread Wellington's ass wider, so Wellington instinctively bent over to allow for easier access. By this time the skinny guard had ripped the lining from the jockstrap more in anxiety than temper as he hadn't been watching what he was doing and was more interested in Wellington's erection. Wellington stared horrified at the torn jockstrap, wondering if the diamonds would fall free and then the game would be up for him.

"Fritz," commanded the burly guard, "go and fetch me some grease of some sort."

The skinny man beetled away in a hurry at which time, Wellington, who was also finding the whole event amusing, said to the burly guard, "I hope he's not coming back because I don't like other people watching when I have sex."

Here was a flicker of realization in the burly guard's eyes and he immediately removed his hand from Wellington and locked the door to the room. He then returned to Wellington and continued where he'd left off, except now he had decided to kneel in front of Wellington with his fingers up Wellington's ass and his mouth clamped firmly on the black ramrod. Wellington stood his ground as loud slurping and sucking sounds came from the burly man's throat. He was thoroughly enjoying the inspection he was undergoing and he could feel himself getting closer and closer to shooting. Should he warn the guard or not, he wondered? Why bother. Let the burly man have a taste of a Black man's juice, he thought. Suddenly his balls rose up and his cock stiffened and a spurt of warm cum shot to the back of the burly guard's throat, causing him to cough. He released his mouth momentarily and received a splash of cum across his face, and then he clamped back onto Wellington's erupting cock, determined not to lose any more juice. As he sucked out the last of the juice, there was a pounding on the door. The burly guard, rushed to unlock the door and there stood Heinz.

Heinz stared at the guard's cum-streaked face, then at the naked Wellington still with his almighty erection and some cum dripping from its tip.

"What is going on in here?" blasted Heinz.

The guard began stammering to explain. He said that he had found marijuana on Wellington and was searching him for more.

"Were you hoping to suck it out of his cock, man? Or dig it out of his ass?"

Heinz was furious. Just then the skinny guard reappeared with a jar of Elbow Grease, marked HOT.

"Here is the cream, Helmut."

On seeing Heinz the skinny guard seemed to disappear inside himself. Heinz took the tub of grease from Fritz, looked at the writing on the jar and added, "Were you hoping to burn it out of him?"

It was clear from Helmut's uniform, that he had developed his own hard-on while he was giving Wellington a blowjob, because a small wet patch had appeared and there was a definite protrusion in the from of his uniform.

"Get out!" shouted Heinz and both Helmut and Fritz disappeared. "I am so sorry for this," said Heinz looking at my torn jockstrap, "and for the humiliation you have undergone."

"It was nothing," said Wellington, still standing naked with a semi-hard erection.

"I'm actually sorry I arrived so late," continued Heinz, "because I might have stopped all this."

"It is a pity," said Wellington, "that you didn't come earlier, not because of the stopping, but I think you make a much more handsome policeman than either of those two."

Heinz blushed profusely, knowing what Wellington was hinting at.

"I don't know if you can wear these again," said Heinz holding up the jockstrap. Maybe I should keep it as a memento of something I never had."

Panic struck Wellington.

"No, I can still wear them. In any case, with this cock of mine, I need underwear to keep it under control, so could I have them back please?"

Heinz reluctantly handed the jockstrap back and Wellington immediately pulled it on to try and cover his still hard cock.

"Jim phoned me and told me what had happened. I think we should lose the marijuana and let you go, if that's agreeable to you?"

"I can't thank you enough."

"Maybe another day you might thank me, especially if you are staying here in Berlin for a few days as Jim says."

"Of definitely," replied Wellington, only too happy to get his clothes on and out of the airport.

When Heinz escorted Wellington through customs and out to his friends, there were obvious signs of relief on their faces, except Wellington's. Heinz organized a cab for them and after Jim had thanked him again and promised to phone, the four set off to their hotel in the Schönberg area.

"Why are you looking so stressed?" asked Jim.

"They tore my jockstrap!"

Panic also seized Jim, but neither he nor Wellington could show it in front of Chad or me.

"We'll see if we can fix it when we get to the hotel," reassured Jim.

Our drive to the center of Berlin didn't take long and we soon found ourselves in Fuggerstrasse approaching our hotel. One thing I will say about Jim's bookings of hotels was that he knew where to book us; near the action. Although it was in the heart of the gay area of Berlin, the street was a hive of activity and noisy as I had expected, but then it was daytime and most people would be at work. We alighted from our cab and booked into the hotel, again Chad and I sharing.

"What happened?" asked Jim when he and Wellington were alone in their room.

"Where are the diamonds? I thought they were in my jockstrap, but when they tore the lining to check for drugs, nothing fell out."

"Well, maybe Mr. Schoonraad made it so well, they wouldn't fall out," replied Jim. "Let's take a look."

Wellington stripped and took off the slightly tattered jockstrap. Jim felt around the studs in the hopes of feeling a rough diamond or two.

"Hm, nice and warm," he said, feeling the inside of the jockstrap, and then he raised it to his nose and sniffed. "It smells delicious as well."

"Cut it out, James. The diamonds."

Jim looked at the torn lining and then got a pair of scissors and tried to probe one of the studs away from the material. After some effort the stud gave way and fell to the floor. There was nothing behind it. Jim and Wellington both looked horrified at each other.

Jim picked up the telephone and dialed our room. I answered and heard his voice.

"Mike, have you guys changed yet?"

"No, Jim, why?"

"Just come round to our room by yourself if you don't mind." The phone was put down and they waited for me.

When I enter their room, there was an awkward moment as Jim tried as best he could to explain what he wanted.

"Uhm, have you still got you jockstrap on, Mike?"

"Yes, why?"

"Well you know how they tore Wellington's jockstrap and I was wondering if you wouldn't mind lending me yours so that we can get another one made like that for Wellington."

"Of course you can, not a problem," I answered taking off my leather jeans and then slipping out of my jockstrap.

I handed the garment to Jim and pulled my jeans back on.

"Is that it?"

"Yes, thanks, kid," replied Jim, and I left.

Jim raised my warm jockstrap to his nose.

"Mm, it smells as delicious as yours – the two men in my life."

"Quick, have a look inside."

Jim got to work with his scissors again sand popped one of the studs. A glittering uncut diamond dropped onto the bed and both men smiled at the same time."

"How come Mike had the jockstrap with the diamonds?" asked Wellington.

"We must have returned the wrong one to him and you had his original jockstrap. Thank God, we did that; otherwise we might both have been in jail tonight."

8

SHOPPING

After we had unpacked and Wellington and Jim were happy to know the diamonds were safe, we all set off to explore Berlin. We had free time on our hands as Jim had informed us that he and Wellington had a business arrangement on Wednesday night. This gave us two free days to do as we pleased, either together or alone. As neither I nor Chad had been to Berlin before, Jim took it upon himself to show us around as though he were the epitome of a tour guide.

"Wouldn't it be easier if we got one of those city bus tours." asked Chad, quietly to me.

"You're probably right there," I agreed.

After hopping on and off trains on the U-Bahn, we eventually arrived at Kochstrasse where we disembarked and walked to Checkpoint Charlie, the dividing point between the old East and West Berlin. We saw the sentry box and then headed in a northerly direction aiming for the famous Unter den Linden Street with its equally famous Brandenburg Gate. All four of us stood in admiration of the sights that we saw and to cool off after our long walk, we headed into the Tiergarten, with its rivers and trees and shade. We spent some time wandering through the parkland checking out the few German boys we could find, we strolled down towards the main Kurfürstendamm Street with its elegant stores and the famous Kaiser-Wilhelm-Gedächtnis-Kirche which stood as a reminder to all of the effects of war. The ruins of this bombed out church left us all in awe of the devastation that war brings to us all. Once we looked at our map that we had acquired, we noticed that we were very near to our hotel, so we all decided to go back and have a rest after the strenuous exercise we had undergone with all the walking. Chad and I collapsed onto our double bed and fell asleep almost instantly. What Wellington and Jim did, I do not know.

Chad woke up first and snuggled up next to me, putting his arm around me and kissing me gently.

"Are you making a move on me or just trying to wake me up?" I mumbled as I opened my eyes.

"Neither, I was just loving you, that's all. I don't think you know how much you make me feel at peace, Mike; just lying here next to you is the greatest feeling ever."

"Ever?" I said with alarm "I thought my making love to you was the greatest ever."

"Well, that too. The only thing that worries me is what is going to happen when I leave."

"What do you mean, when you leave? You're not going anywhere."

"But I have to go back to Toronto and you don't know how much longer you're touring Europe, and I can't expect you guys to fund everything for me."

"Hey, listen. As long as I'm here, you'll be here."

"Do you think the others are awake, that's if they had a sleep?" asked Chad.

"Let's give them a call."

I picked up the telephone and rang their room. Wellington answered.

"Are you guys awake?"

"No, this is me talking in my sleep. Of course we're awake; we're not faders like you two who can't take the pace. What are you guys up to?"

"Nothing," I answered.

"Liar, you're probably attacking that tight little ass of Chad's as we speak."

"How would you know if it's tight, hey?"

"It looks it," replied Wellington.

"Well you're right there," I replied. "So what's happening tonight?"

"We're going to the hotel's club. Do you want to join us?"

"Sounds fine to me and I'm sure Chad won't object."

"What won't I object to?" asked Chad, butting into my and Wellington's conversation.

I covered the mouthpiece of the phone.

"They're going to the club here in the hotel. Do you want to go?"

Chad nodded.

"Shall we meet you downstairs?"

"OK, then we can go and have something to eat first. I'll see you in about an hour's time."

The phone then went dead.

"We're meeting them downstairs in an hour's time, so climb into that shower and beautify yourself," I said, giving Chad a gentle slap on his ass.

When we got downstairs, Wellington and Jim had only just arrived there.

"There is a message for you, sir," said the receptionist to Jim.

He unfolded the piece of paper and read the instructions to himself.

"Excuse me, but do you have a map handy, please?" he asked the receptionist.

"Certainly sir, here you are," replied the young man, handing a map book to Jim.

Jim and Wellington huddled a little way away from us and mumbled to each other so that we wouldn't hear them.

"It says we must get off at the Schörhauser Allee U-Bahn, walk in a north direction until we reach Rodenbergstrasse, and then turn right. Go to number 23. Schwarz Zimmer (sex party). What do you think the 'sex party' means, or the Schwarz Zimmer?" asked Jim.

"I don't know, but maybe the receptionist here knows."

Jim crossed over to the reception desk and called the young man.

"I'm sorry to trouble you, but who brought this message for me?"

"A young skinhead, about early twenties. Looked a bit rough, but clean."

"Did he say anything else to you?"

"No sir."

"And can you tell me what this might mean, in the note it says, 'sex party'. Do you understand what it might mean?"

The young man's face lit up with delight.

"It means just that, sir. There's to be a sex party. May I ask where, sir?"

"The note just says we are to go to some street and it's got Schwarz Zimmer on the note."

"Oh ja, that is the name of a club. I know it well. When are you going?"

"Wednesday."

"In that case the sex party will be underwear," replied the young man. "On Wednesday it is underwear and on Fridays it is naked parties."

"What a pity we aren't going on a Friday," said Wellington, shrugging his shoulders in despair.

Chad and I became impatient with Jim spending all his time at reception, so we went over to see what the problem was.

"What's going on?" I asked, but never got a proper answer"

"Come on let's go and get something to eat," said Jim heading for the exit and the rest of us following him.

When we returned from having a dinner of German sausages and sauerkraut, which none of us enjoyed, we found the club at the hotel pumping with loud music and a lively crowd of men dancing and drinking. We joined in and spent an entertaining evening learning how German men party and play although as far as I knew none of us ventured into the club's darkroom for a bit of excitement.

———————

The following day, Chad and I decided to go for some retail therapy. Wellington and Jim, on the other hand, decided to chill out and take a day trip to see the Schönberg Palace, so after breakfast they left. Chad and I decided to go to Motzstrasse to check out a leather store to buy some more leather items, but before we left Chad and I tried on each other's leather garments in our bedroom.

"Chad let me try your harness on; I'd like to see what it's like with the cock ring attachment."

Chad put it on me and then I pushed my balls through the metal ring, which was a bit of a struggle, but the real struggle came when I tried to get my cock through. Perseverance is the key word and with much pulling and pushing, and my cock getting a little harder, everything fitted through.

"Wow, it really pushes your balls and cock up and out, hey! But it's a great feeling. I think I must get one," I said excitedly.

"Why get one Mike, why not just buy the attachment."

"What do you mean?"

"You should be able to get a leather attachment with the cock ring on and it's press-studded to the other part of the harness."

"Hey, that's ideal then. And the shorts, can I try them as well?"

We managed to get my semi-hard cock and balls out of the cock ring and the harness off, then Chad helped me into his shorts.

"It's pretty handy to have the same size waist, and then we can share things," I added.

"I like the word share," replied Chad with a grin.

We pulled on the shorts and then zipped them up. Chad ran his hand over my ass and licked his lips as he did so.

"Nice tight fit, hey? Maybe I could unzip you and slip my cock into you like you threatened to do to me."

"When did I threaten?"

"Well not actually threatened but you suggested how nice it could be if we were dancing together for example."

"Oh yes, I do remember, but I still haven't had a chance to do that to you."

"By the way, if you don't want the shorts in leather, I know you can get them in rubber," suggested Chad.

"You're quite a kinky guy aren't you?"

"You know what I'd like to get is a jockstrap like yours with the studs on. I think it's so sexy looking," said Chad.

"That reminds me, Wellington still has mine. I must get it back from him."

"But they've already left for their tour," replied Chad.

"Oh hell. Maybe I could get the maid to open their room for me and I can get it. Let me go and see if I can find one who might be making up the rooms."

I wandered off and did find one and with much persuasion, she eventually opened up their room for me. I went in and found two similar jockstraps lying on the dressing table, so I thought they had replaced the damaged one and took mine, and as I was leaving my eye caught a piece of paper next to the jockstraps. Now I'm not usually inquisitive, but something made me pick up the paper because I thought it looked like the paper that Jim was given by the receptionist. On it I read the message about the 'darkroom' and 'sex party'. I replaced the paper and headed back to Chad.

"Here we go," said as I entered our room. "Slip this on and let's see what you look like all studded."

Chad stripped off his clothes and put on the studded jockstrap.

"It sure gives you support and it looks incredibly sexy," he added, rubbing his hand across the studded pouch. "I didn't realize that the pouch was quite heavy, probably from the studs, but just the feel of this could give me a hard-on."

"So are you getting one?"

"Do you mean hard-on or jockstrap?"

"Both," I joked.

"Yeah, I think I'm going to buy one or one of those with a zip in the front pouch."

"You really like easy access to your vital parts of your body, hey?"

We both giggled as we thought how kinky we both were.

"Come on, Chad, take it off and let's head to do some shopping."

We went in search of the leather store in Motzstrasse that the receptionist had told us about and found it very easily. We went in to an array of exciting leather and rubber items. A tall, slim German with a goatee and small moustache came up to us.

"Guten morgen," he said, cheerfully.

"I'm sorry, I don't speak German," I replied.

"I am sorry, how may I help you?"

"We're looking for some leather items, for both of us. My friend here was looking for a jockstrap with studs on, do you have?"

He went over to a rack that was filled with various types of leather jockstraps and posing pouches. He took one and showed it to Chad.

"This one has a double pouch, zipped and a cock ring."

"You mean all in one?" asked Chad.

"Yes, sir. What size are you?"

"About a 32 inch waist, please."

"Here we are, sir. Would you like to try it on? The change room is over there," he said pointing to a couple of cubicles situated close to the rack.

Chad went off to try on his jockstrap leaving me with the salesman.

"For me I'm looking for an attachment to my harness that has a cock ring. Do you know what I mean?"

"Over here, sir."

He took me to the other side of the store where the harnesses were hanging.

"Which type of harness do you have, sir?"

I looked through the ones hanging there, found a similar one and pointed it out to him.

"For that model, we do have an attachment."

He picked up a length of leather with a metal ring attached at one end.

"This end is clipped to your harness so it can be removed at any time," he said. "Would you also like to try this?"

"Thanks very much," I answered and made my way to the cubicle next to Chad's.

The salesman then went back to Chad.

"How does that fir, sir?"

Chad opened the door to his cubicle to show the salesman. Without batting an eye, the salesman knelt in front of Chad and began to check that all fitted well. Chad watched as the man felt to see if the waist was not too tight, then he ran his finger tips under the sides that ran between Chad's crotch to see that it cupped his balls properly. Throughout this, Chad could feel himself getting aroused. Then the salesman gently placed his hand on the actual pouch.

"Is there sufficient room in there for you sir?" he asked, looking up at Chad.

"I think so, "replied Chad, but the hand remained there.

"Perhaps sir would like something a little bigger? We have others that are the same waist size but the pouches are made for bigger men."

"Maybe I should try that," answered Chad. "Also, I think if I'm wearing my harness with the cock ring I won't need a jockstrap with a built-in cock ring."

"Not a problem, sir," said the salesman rising and going to fetch Chad another jockstrap.

When he returned, he handed Chad the new jockstrap and also checked on me and found me standing naked in front of the cubicle mirror with the harness and cock ring on.

"How's that sir?"

He looked in the mirror and saw my hefty cock semi-hard while my balls had swollen too. His eyes smiled at the sight and then I saw him admiring my naked ass.

"Does it feel comfortable, sir."

I turned to face him.

"I like the way it lifts your cock and balls," I said casually, allowing the young man to view what was on display.

I could see that his mouth was getting dry as he constantly licked his lips and his hands became fidgety. I was sure that he wanted to touch, but didn't know where.

"If you need a bigger ring, we can supply that, sir."

"I don't know, what do you think?"

"It depends on how much the ring is strangling your balls and cock, sir."

I knew he was dying to touch, so I egged him on.

"Do you think there should be more space between the ring and my cock for example?"

The salesman's finger shook as he neared the ring. He then placed a finger on my cock and tried to slide his finger under the metal ring – it was tight. He then moved his finger to my balls and did likewise there.

"It seems a bit tight, sir, but it's what you want."

By now I had a full erection and my cock was throbbing gently. His eyes were glued to my cock's movement and his lips were drying out completely. I eased forward slightly as if to encourage him to open his mouth. My cock was now about three inches away from his face. Temptation got the better of him and our young German salesman opened his mouth. I felt his warm breath on my shaft and then his dry lips clamped firmly around my thick shaft. He slowly and silently sank his mouth down my length until his chin reached my balls then he sucked and began to draw his mouth along the length until he reached the tip where he prodded my piss slit with his tongue tip.

"That feels lovely," I whispered, hoping Chad wouldn't hear.

As I spoke he must have realized what he was doing because he suddenly leapt to his feet, adjusted his erection that he'd developed in his leathers and exited my cubicle. I turned and smiled into the mirror. I then peeped out of the cubicle door and saw the salesman trying to compose himself behind the counter.

"How are you doing, Chad?" I called to the cubicle next door.

"Fun," he replied. "And you?"

"Let's just say it's entertaining."

"Mike check this out. What do you think of this jockstrap?"

"I can't come out; I haven't got any clothes on."

"What! Have you been having sex in there?"

"Not yet. You come here."

Chad wandered out of his cubicle and opened the door to mine. He saw me standing naked with the harness and cock ring on, and then he saw my hard-on.

"No wonder you didn't want to come out. What caused that?"

"The cock ring, and the salesman," I replied with a grin.

"You too?"

"Yeah, actually he's got a good mouth and knows how to use it. How about you?"

"I've just had the gentle touch."

"Here he comes again," I said shutting the cubicle door and Chad beetling back into his cubicle.

He opened the door to my cubicle and asked, "Is there anything else I could bring you sir?"

I turned to talk to him, still naked and with a semi-hard-on.

"There is something else I'm looking for and that's a pair of shorts but the kind with a zip that extends from the back to the front. Do you have something like that?"

"Yes, sir, but not in leather. I have some in rubber if you're interested."

"Sure, could you bring me a couple of pairs? I've never worn rubber before so I don't know if the sizes remain the same or not."

"Usually rubber is a much tighter fit, sir, so should I bring you three sizes, maybe a 32, 34 and 36 inch?"

I smiled back at our salesman.

"You know best."

With that he disappeared but was back hastily thrusting the shorts at me as I busily removed the harness.

"I f you say that rubber is tighter, I think you might have to help me get into these shorts," I proposed.

He stepped into the cubicle and closed the door behind him. As I bent over to step into the first pair of shorts, my ass rubbed against his crotch and I could feel a solid piece of meat there. I stood up and tried to zip up, but the waist was too tight for me to button.

"Too small," I said, again bending over to remove them.

He handed me the next pair which I stepped into and zipped up.

"Wow, you're right about being tight."

"It's meant to enhance your attributes," he answered, not that my attributes needed any more enhancing.

"What do you think?" I asked turning to face him.

He studied my front and back then he said, "May I try the zip, sir?"

I stood facing the mirror while the salesman slowly and carefully began unzipping from the back. The sound of the zip was all that could be heard as it slid over my ass crack.

"Could you spread your legs, sir?"

I did so and the salesman knelt behind me as his hand slid the zipper between my thighs and he carefully let his hand run between my legs so that I could feel my balls resting on his arm. Without turning me around, he continued unzipping and I could feel his hand ride over my swollen cock. When the zip was fully undone and he had ample access to my cock, his hand clamped onto my shaft and he began a slow stroking motion. In doing so, he removed my cock from the confines of the rubber and continued to jack me off. His hands were soft to the touch and his slow rhythmic up and down strokes were electric to me. Slowly I turned to face him and when I had turned around, he smiled up at me and both his hand and his mouth began to work me over. The fact that I was being sucked and jacked off by a handsome leather guy and in the close confines of the cubicle in a public place, was a complete turn on for me and I knew that, although I usually lasted a long time before shooting my load, this was going to be over very quickly. I was right.

"I'm gonna shoot," I whispered.

He held his mouth at the tip of my cock waiting for the first load to be expelled, but continued to jack me off.

"Ugh!" I grunted as the first salvo fired into his mouth, quickly followed by another and another load until I was writhing in ecstasy as he sucked me dry.

When he had done so, he kissed the tip of my cock, stood up and smiled at me.

"You can try the other pair on if you like sir, but I think these will do the job for you. I'd better get back to your friend, sir."

In our ecstasy I think we'd both forgotten Chad waiting in the next door cubicle.

The salesman opened the door to Chad's cubicle.

"Can I get you anything else, sir?"

"Yes. Please come in and close the door," said Chad.

As the salesman did so, Chad, who was still wearing his jockstrap pulled the salesman to him and kissed him on the mouth. As he did this, his hand dropped down to the salesman's crotch and he felt the stiff cock waiting to be dealt with. His fingers took hold of the zip and undid it, and then he slipped his hand into the warm leather jeans and found the long, thin cock with its wet tip. Chad pulled it free from the leather and left the salesman's lips. Chad smiled at him then sank to his knees.

"I heard you next door and I want to treat you like you treated my friend."

Chad eyed the uncut cock and gripping the shaft, he pushed the man's foreskin back until the rosy pink head appeared, then he licked around the tip, digging his tongue into the opening. The salesman groaned but that didn't deter Chad. Chad's tongue licked along the underneath of his shaft and reached the man's balls. Gently he sucked each into his mouth until both fitted in tightly. Chad let his tongue salivate over them in his mouth, and then he spat them out and licked his way back up to the tip again. On his second journey along the hard shaft, he sank his mouth over the tip and sucked, then slid his mouth down the man's length, opening up his throat to allow for depth. Chad continued this for some time until the salesman took hold of Chad's head to hold it still, and started to face-fuck Chad. Chad realized that the man was obviously close to coming, so he readied himself for the onslaught. He didn't have long to wait. With audible gasps and groans, the salesman fired into Chad's throat. The young customer swallowed as quickly as was possible as the salesman continued to thrust his cock into Chad's mouth. Finally, Chad released his grip on the salesman's cock, pulled it again to his mouth and watched as the foreskin came back to cover the rose-pink head and out came the last remaining drops of cum which Chad licked away. The salesman then placed his hands under Chad's arms and lifted him. Their mouths met and the salesman could taste the remnants of his salty cum in Chad's mouth and using his tongue tried to extract it as best he could, then he zipped up his leather jeans smiled at Chad and left the cubicle. By that time, I was waiting outside for them both.

Chad and I paid for out items, having received a hefty discount, and made our way back to the hotel which was nearby. Neither of us said a word until we got up to the room.

"Well, how was it for you?" asked Chad.

"Good. No very good."

"Better than me?"

"Never! And for you?" I asked.

"I enjoyed his cock," replied Chad, "But nothing compared to yours."

"But what about you?"

"I heard you guys at it and it made me horny and I knew that you had shot your load, so when he came into my cubicle I could see how frustrated he was at not coming, so I thought I'd treat him like he treated you. So no, I didn't come."

I felt awful when Chad told me that and promised to make it up to him, because I honestly thought that the guy had treated Chad the same way that I was treated.

9

DISCOVERY

Wednesday evening arrived and Jim and Wellington were busy planning for their 'business meeting' as they had told Chad and me.

"You boys remember I told you Wellington and I have a meeting tonight."

"No we haven't forgotten," I replied.

"So what are you guys planning on doing tonight?"

"I don't know. We haven't spoken about it, but if you're going out, we might too. Maybe even wear some of our new leather outfits we bought yesterday."

"You didn't tell us about those. What did you get?"

"I got myself an attachment for my harness; you know the ones with the cock ring attached?"

"Oh yes, those are rather nice," answered Jim.

"And a pair of shorts like Chad's except mine are in rubber and not leather like his."

"Rubber, hey? The kid's getting kinky," remarked Wellington.

"And he looks incredibly sexy in them," said Chad, interrupting my story.

"And you, Chad, what did you get?" asked Jim.

"A jockstrap like Mike's. I like all those studs; they look so manly and rough."

"Oh, so you're into a bit of rough, are you?" quipped Wellington.

"Not really, but I don't mind a bit occasionally," retorted Chad.

"Now he tells me," I answered.

"What else?" enquired Jim.

"Nothing, but it certainly was fun trying on all the different things," I volunteered, without giving them the juicy details of what had happened in the cubicles.

"Well, we're going to get changed for our meeting and no doubt we'll see you guys in the morning, so enjoy whatever you do tonight," said Jim, ushering us out of their room.

Suddenly Jim had a flash

"I've just thought of something," said Jim after we'd departed.

"And what's that?" asked Wellington.

"This place we're going to tonight, according to the receptionist has an underwear only night on a Wednesday, so how are we going to carry and hand over the diamonds?" asked Jim.

"Easy, I'm wearing the jockstrap with the studs as my underwear. I've already placed the diamond in the hollowed out studs, so it's not a problem."

"So you're telling me you're going to go whoring around in the most expensive jockstrap on earth?"

"That's right. How else are we going to hide them if we've only got underwear on?"

"That's why I love you and need you, Duke. So what do I wear?"

"Whatever you fancy. It actually won't matter as I'll have the gems safe next to my body."

"And the money? How do we get that out if we're all running around half naked?" asked Jim.

"I don't know, but I suppose they have the same problem as we did. Where do they put the money, unless it's stuffed into their jocks?"

"And another thing, how will we know who we're dealing with?"

"Leave that to me James. I have a pretty good idea who the person could be."

Jim and Wellington then dressed. Wellington put on the jockstrap that lay next to the slip of paper with the address on, and his blue jeans, while Jim pulled on a pair of white Calvin Klein briefs and then his denim jeans. They then headed off to the nearest underground station to catch the train to their destination.

In the meantime, Chad and I had decided to visit a local club near to the hotel, called Scheune, so we were busy getting our outfits sorted out.

"Tell me, Mike, what exactly does Jim do?"

"You mean work wise?"

"Yes."

"You know, I don't really know. All I know is that he has a very up-market apartment in Chelsea in London, can afford to keep Wellington and travels a great deal. Admittedly he doesn't have a family to support, but all I know is that it has something to do with finance, but what, that I can't say. Why do you ask?"

"It's just that he said they were going to a business meeting and I wondered what sort of work he did that warranted a meeting at night and with Wellington."

"You're quite the little detective, aren't you, Chad boy?"

"Hey not so little; I'm about as big as you."

"Now, now. Let's not get into that discussion or do you want me to get the tape measure out and we can measure each other's cocks?"

"So what are you going to wear, Mike?"

"I thought my new shorts, but I also like my studded jockstrap, except the two together won't go; and you?"

"I thought my harness and my new jockstrap with the zip in the front."

"Oh I see, I'm wearing the shorts with the zip in the front and back and you've got the jocks with the zip in the front, so are you intending to dance with me so you can unzip my back and your front and then slip you hard dick into my ass? Is that the plan?"

"You know, I never thought of that, but shit that's a bloody good idea. Come here."

Chad grabbed me, spun me around so my back was to him and he pushed his crotch up against my bare ass, and then placed his hands on my studded pouch.

"Oh yes, I could get to like this," he giggled as I felt his thrusts against my ass crack.

As he was playing around, something caught my eye lying on the carpet of the room.

"Hang on, Chad," I said, breaking away from his grasp.

"What's it?"

I bent down and picked up one of the studs from my jockstrap and next to it on the carpet was a shining glass-looking object.

"What's that Mike?"

"Well this is a stud from my jocks but I don't know what this other thing is."

Chad took the glass-looking object from me, studied it and then announced that it was a diamond.

"Ah, don't be stupid. Where's a diamond come from?"

"I'm telling you, Mike this is a diamond, and what makes it worse is that it's an uncut one. It's illegal to carry uncut diamonds, so where do you think it's come from?"

"I've no idea, but why would the stud come off as well?"

"Mike, take off your jockstrap for me, please."

Chad sat down on the bed and took the jockstrap when I had taken it off. He studied it carefully and fiddled with one or two of the studs. As he was fiddling with a stud, it popped off onto the bed and another uncut diamond fell from the hollowed out area with in the stud.

"I hope I'm wrong about this, Mike, but there's another diamond here. Perhaps someone's hidden them under these studs to smuggle them somewhere."

Chad continued slowly and carefully dismantling a few more studs and under each we found a diamond.

"Oh my God!" I exclaimed, "Now things might be beginning to make sense."

"Why? What's going through your mind?"

"You know when I went to Jim and Wellington's room to get my jockstrap…"

"…yes."

"Well I saw a piece of paper and I read it. It didn't make much sense at the time, but these diamonds might be linked to that piece of paper."

"Now who's being the little detective?" quipped Chad.

"Honey, I'm a big detective, and you should know that. Seriously though, I think this has something to do with Jim and the meeting tonight might be to hand over the diamonds or sell them to someone."

"But how could it? The diamonds are still here. They haven't taken them."

"No, because when I went into their room there were two jockstraps and I picked up this one. Maybe mine was the other one and I took the wrong thing, which would mean that if one of them is wearing the other jockstrap, they think they have the diamonds with them, but instead we have them here. Oh shit!"

"So where did they have to go according to the piece of paper?"

"It said something about Schönhauser Allee U-Bahn. Then there was an instruction to walk in a northerly direction, I think, until they reached Rodenbergstrasse or something like that, and then turn right. That I remember. Then there was a number, which I can't remember. At the bottom of the paper it said something Zimmer (sex party)."

"That's all very well, but what's the Zimmer and sex party got to do with the diamonds?"

"I don't know, but what I do know is that if they have gone to their so-called meeting without the diamonds, they could be heading for trouble, so I think we should forget the club and go and find them. What do you think?"

"I agree, but hang on. Didn't the young guy at reception give them a piece of paper? Maybe he can give us some help here?"

"Good idea, babes. Let's go down and ask him."

We quickly made our way down to reception and found the young man.

"Excuse us, sir but you know our friends, the big Black guy and the older man...?"

"Yes."

"You gave them a note that was hand delivered here."

"Yes, a young skinhead guy brought it."

"Right," I said, as though I knew that information. "But can you tell us how we get to the address and what is the Zimmer and sex party?"

"Oh are you also going?"

"Yes," I said enthusiastically, "But we don't know what to expect."

"Tonight is underwear night, as I told your friends. The Schwarz Zimmer is a club."

"And it's underwear only?"

"Yes."

"Thank you so much. Come Chad let's go back up stairs and get ready."

We ran up the stairs rather than wait for the lift to arrive.

"Now it makes sense to me," I said. "I would imagine that Wellington was going to wear the jockstrap with the removable studs because they would only be allowed to wear underwear in the club and that would be how they could carry the diamonds. Put on some underwear, Chad and help me to replace the studs that have popped off; then we must get the underground to the club.

We hastily replaced the studs, placing the uncut diamonds back in their hollows. I pulled on the studded jockstrap with the diamonds and then pulled on my leather jeans. Chad had put on his 2Xist briefs and his denim jeans and off we went.

10

SKINHEAD BANG

The train journey seemed to take forever, and the whole way I was worrying about the safety of Jim and Wellington. We were in a foreign country and although I liked the German's I had met, I didn't know what other types of people there might be, especially those types who dealt in illicit diamond smuggling. We finally arrived at the designated station and got off the train. When we exited the station we didn't know which way was north.

"Excuse me, sir," I asked the first man I saw. "I'm looking for the Darkroom club; do you know where it is?"

He pointed in a particular direction and told us to go about three blocks, which we did. We came to a street which, in the dark, we found to be the correct street.

"Turn right," I said.

"There," shouted Chad. "I see a sign with Darkroom written on it."

We ran to the building and on reaching it paid to go in. We were given a locker each in which to place our clothes and leave our underwear and boots on.

"How the hell are we going to find them in this place?" asked Chad, as we ventured into a dimly lit bar area.

"Just keep your eyes open, Chad."

We looked around the bar area and didn't see wither Jim or Wellington. Music was blaring and men in their underwear were scattered around the bar area. There were some in jockstraps, some in briefs and some even in G-strings, each man showing off his assets. I went up to the bar counter and spoke to one of the barmen.

"Hi, we're tourists and new here. Where is everything?"

The young barman looked me up and down before answering, but seemed to ignore Chad. I noticed how his eyes fixated on my studded crotch.

"I will show you around," he said in a fairly sullen way, and removed himself from behind the bar counter.

He led us down a short corridor and into another fairly spacious room where men were dancing. We searched for Jim but didn't see him.

"This is dance area," said the barman.

Although he was young and reasonably attractive, it was his voice and sullen approach that put me off.

From the dance area, we went though another door and down a longer corridor off which led a number of rooms. The first we went into, we were told was the piss room and a couple of guys were busy enjoying a golden shower. Next we made our way into a double sling room. I say double because there were two slings in the same room. Both were occupied and both had a gathering of men around each sling. Chad and I moved closer to see if either Wellington or Jim might be in the sling. In the one was a large dark-haired man who was being fisted by those around him while a couple took turns in shoving their cocks into his gaping mouth. In the other sling was a young slim guy of about early twenties. His legs were spread wide and five men were taking it in turn to fuck him. He seemed to be enjoying each one of them, and so was I, just watching. As I stood there transfixed as they took turns, I felt a hand on my naked ass and a finger slip quickly into my chute. I gasped as the finger entered me and turned to see who it was. The barman stood next to me, his face emotionless as his fingers dug deeper into my chute. Although his fingers had hit my prostate and the feeling was sending my cock into orbit, I needed to find Jim first. Without being impolite, I turned to him, grabbed his crotch and felt his hard cock, then whispered, "Later you can have it."

All the while I was anxious in case anyone grabbed my crotch and dislodged the hidden diamonds.

"Where to next?" I asked.

Our guide led us into the other rooms, which had a maze and a darkroom with mattresses scattered around the floor and some rooms had candles flickering and mirrors around the walls. There was also a shower area and obviously the toilets. We looked everywhere and didn't see Jim or Wellington.

As we headed back to the bar, I asked our guide if he had seen any Black guys tonight.

He glanced at me and nodded his head.

"A big guy," he said.

I knew that would be Wellington.

"Is he still here?"

I could see the look of disdain in the barman's face. It was look of 'What do you want with a Black guy when I can have you'. I didn't want to say we were friends in case it jeopardized Wellington's situation.

"He's upstairs in the loft," replied the barman.

"I'd really like to see him. I hear he's like a giant and has a massive cock on him too," I added.

"No-one can go up there."

"But why, is it a private area?"

"Yes."

"Oh please, can't I see this guy?"

It wasn't getting me anywhere, so Chad and I ordered a drink and sat down to plan. At least we knew that if Wellington was there, so would Jim.

"Chad I really don't like to do this to you, but I need you to help me. I've got to get up to this loft area and see what's going on, but I don't know how to get there."

"So what's the plan?"

"I really hate saying this, but the barman fancies my ass, and I was wondering…"

"…yes?"

"I was wondering if you could keep him occupied while I tried to find a way up to the loft."

"So are you offering me up as a sacrifice?"

"To a nice young German boy; what could be better than that?"

"You know you make it sound so irresistibly nice. So what do you want me to do?"

"Well that's up to you whether you want the sling room or the piss room or anything else."

"Oh great."

"I'm going to tell him that my boyfriend fancies him and wants to have a scene with him and see what happens."

We walked over to the bar with our drinks and waited for the young barman to come to us.

"Hi, my friend; what's your name?" I asked.

He stared at me like some drug-induced animal, and then answered, "Heinrich".

"Well Heinrich," I continued, whispering, "My friend here likes you and he would like to go with you for a short time. He's got a cute tight ass and a big cock as well. Would you be interested and then maybe later I'll be free."

Heinrich looked at Chad, leaned over the bar to check out the size of the package in the 2Xist briefs, and then said, "Turn around."

Chad did his modeling turn for the young guy to see his ass and then Heinrich, with a sigh, said, "OK, go to the sling room, I'll be there as soon as I can. Wait for me there. If a sling is vacant, get in but don't let anyone else touch you."

I thought they were very simple and direct instructions, so Chad and I made our way to the sling room. By this time it was empty, so Chad climbed into the sling but keeping his briefs on.

"Good luck Mike and be careful."

"I will\, and you too," I said, as I left him there and went back to the bar area.

I sat in a darkened area and watched Heinrich. At one point I noticed he looked up and as I followed his eyes, I saw a young shaven-headed man. I wondered if he was the skinhead that the receptionist had spoken of. I then traced the view across the upper roof and finally I saw a staircase. At the same time, I saw Heinrich leave the bar counter, but his friend upstairs was obviously acting as watch while he was away. I crept to where I had seen the stairway and began to ascend the iron steps as quietly as I could.

In the sling room Heinrich had arrived to find Chad waiting for him. He moved to the side of the sling and unzipped hi jeans. It was apparent that the staff could keep their clothes on but not the customers. Chad turned to face Heinrich's crotch and watched as his long, thick cock emerged. Chad was amazed to think such a scrawny guy had such a thick cock, but it looked appetizing, so Chad willingly open his mouth to take it right in. Heinrich enjoyed the way that Chad's mouth worked on his length and the more that Chad lubricated it, the thicker and longer it grew. When Heinrich felt he was ready, he ripped off Chad's briefs, spread his legs, aimed his cock and moved in.

As the bulbous head of Heinrich's cock touched Chad's pucker, he gasped and felt the slow determined forward push. The young meat sank slowly into the warm confines of Chad's ass and as soon as Heinrich had broken through the tight sphincter muscle, he rammed it all in.

"Aargh!" cried Chad but the pain wasn't intense, it was more the shock of the guy's cock invading his ass so rapidly.

Heinrich started a quick and deep thrust pattern while he held onto the chains attaching the sling to the ceiling. As Chad lay there feeling the young man's cock stretching his chute and bringing him intense pleasure, he thought of Mike and realized that he had to slow the guy down to give Mike time.

"Oh Heinrich slow down, I want to feel you deep inside of me. Push it in and keep it there then pull out and do it again."

Surprisingly Heinrich listened and slowed right down. Although Chad had said it to give Mike more time, he was surprised how good it felt when Heinrich did slow down. In fact it was bringing him closer quicker. Heinrich's thick stem slid deep along Chad's chute, massaging his prostate as it did so. He could see stars in front of him as the young man ground his bulbous cock in and out of the tightness that encircled it. Even the look on Heinrich's face had changed to one of desire and pleasure. A slight smiled emerged as he neared his own climax and when he was about to come, he grabbed Chad's throbbing cock and jacked him off.

There was no verbal warning that he was about to come, but Chad sensed Heinrich's immanent explosion so he clamped his chute tighter almost strangling the young man's shaft.

"Uuurgh!" groaned Heinrich as he sank his cock long and deep, keeping it rammed in Chad's ass while he fired his young German juice. His breathing was loud and heavy and he jacked Chad's cock faster until Chad fired onto his stomach and moaned with pleasure. With each load that Chad fired, so his ass clamped around Heinrich's cock and each time, Heinrich just groaned louder and louder until his body shuddered. When he was expended, Heinrich, holding onto his long thick shaft, slowly pulled out of Chad and watched as the excess cum oozed out of Chad's ass. Heinrich rubbed the head of his circumcised cock over the entrance to Chad's ass allowing some of his cum to saturate his cock and inserted his cock head again into the opening. He continued doing this for about three minutes, driving Chad insane with pleasure, feeling the enlarged head teasing his pucker, breaking the entrance and just entering the chute each time. No one had ever done that to Chad before and although the young man looked inexperienced, Chad was convinced that this was no ordinary young man; here was someone who had used his cock many times before and knew how to please a man.

While Chad lay in the throws of orgasmic ecstasy as a result of his lesson in post sex cock play from the young, virile Heinrich, I continued my stealthy approach to the loft area. When I reached the landing, I saw a door about ten feet from the top of the stairs and next to it was a window. I crept silently towards the window, but didn't see the skinhead |I had seen earlier. Suddenly a voice boomed out over the sound of the music that was beating downstairs.

"You lie!" shouted the German accent.

I then heard Jim's voice.

"Trust me, we're not lying. We did get the diamonds, but we don't have them here."

"If you don't produce them, I'll slit his throat," said the German accent.

I neared the window and ducked down so as not to be seen. Slowly I raised my head to peer through the window. There was a table and two chairs in the room and in each chair sat Wellington and Jim. They both looked extremely vulnerable in their underwear and I noticed that Wellington had on the studded jockstrap, but obviously not the one with the diamonds hidden in it. Next to him stood a young looking skinhead in a pair of faded blue jeans which looked almost white they had faded so much. These jeans were skin tight and were held up by a pair of red bracers. On his chest he had on a white vest that looked a little tattered but it showed off his slightly muscular frame. I had no weapon with which to attack their captor and I wasn't sure if there wasn't someone else involved as well. As I contemplated my next move, I spotted a fire extinguisher adjacent to the wall with the door in, so I crept along and took it off of the wall, then crept back to the window.

"I have warned you enough times, so this is your last warning. Where are the diamonds or he dies?"

I raised my head slightly and looked through the window once more, but this time, Jim spotted me. I raised my finger to my lips to warn him to be quiet, which he understood. I could see the blade of a switchblade knife held at Wellington's throat, ready to slit it, but I wasn't sure whether to attack straight away or wait. My better judgment told me to attack. I burst through the door, spraying foam from the fire extinguisher and hitting the young skinhead in the face with it. Not to be content with that, I smashed the extinguisher against his head, knocking him unconscious.

"What took you so long?" was Wellington's answer to my heroics.

"Listen; in future tell me what you're up to. You could have got killed."

"Untie us, Mike," appealed Jim, "Quickly before someone else comes."

I raced over to Jim and untied him, then the used the rope that had bound him to tie up the young skinhead. I then crossed to Wellington who actually looked quite sexy all tied up.

"Have you ever thought of doing a bit of bondage, Duke?"

"Just untie me before he comes round and attacks again."

"Not until I've had a bit of fun with you."

I moved up close to Wellington and sat down astride his well-built thighs. I could feel his massive bulge resting snugly against my ass.

"Hm! This feels so comfortable. Now if you can pop each stud while I sit on your hefty crotch, you win a prize.

"Come on, get off me," Pleaded Wellington.

"I told you, not until you've popped some studs."

"I'll pop more than studs in a minute," reprimanded Wellington.

"Hey, hey, just remember who saved you."

I ground my ass over his bulging crotch and felt a stirring in his jockstrap.

"A little more and I might get you to pop a stud."

Wellington struggled to break free, but it was useless. The more he struggled, the harder his cock began to feel against my ass.

"I really do think you're about to pop a stud, Duke," I said, grinding my ass hard onto his cock. "Ooh that feels good."

"Come on Mike, give the guy a break; he's had a hard time."

"No harder than I'm getting at the moment," I replied with a satisfied grin on my face.

I rose from Wellington and between Jim and me, we untied him.

"Now what do we do?" asked Jim.

"Tie him to the chair," said Wellington, anger in his voice, "then we get out of here."

"Not before I have answers," I said, firmly.

We tied up the young skinhead, who by now had come round from being knocked unconscious, and then I stood in front of Jim and Wellington to ask my questions.

"I don't want to know why you did this, but I do want to know where the money is?"

"We don't know" said Jim.

I then turned to the skinhead.

"Where's the money for the diamonds?"

He just glared at me, angry because I had hit him.

"Tell me, do you work in this club?"

He nodded.

"So you see plenty of cocks around here?"

Again he nodded.

"And to get to fuck some of the asses that you see here?"

The nod came again.

"And do any of the cocks you see, get to touch your ass?"

He shook his head.

"Oh I see, so you value your ass?"

Again he nodded.

"In that case, tell us where the money is."

Silence.

"I'm sorry to do this to you, and I know how much you treasure your ass, but I'm going to have to sort you out again."

Fear suddenly appeared in his eyes.

"Duke, would you mind taking off your jockstrap, please."

Wellington knew what was coming, so he obliged. He removed his studded jockstrap and stood naked in front of the skinhead, whose eyes had grown wide as he saw the size of Wellington's cock, which was still semi-hard from my grinding ass on his crotch.

"The money?" I asked again.

Silence.

"OK Wellington, he's all yours."

Wellington moved up close to the young man and, holding his cock in his hand rubbed across the young man's face and mouth.

"Open wide," commanded Wellington.

The young skinhead tried to avoid Wellington's cock, but he more he tried the more Wellington held the guy's head still. Eventually the mouth opened and Wellington sank his cock into its warmth.

"Bite it and I kill you," said Wellington, as he started thrusting his cock down the skinhead's throat.

This continued for sometime until Wellington felt his cock was hard and ready for action, and then he physically lifted the skinhead out of the chair, dropped him on the floor and knelt beside him.

"Now I'm gonna fuck you," he hissed.

The young man quivered on the ground as he felt Wellington's cock head nudge his ass hole.

"I'll tell you. I'll tell you."

Wellington held his position.

"Where is it?"

There's a box downstairs behind the counter, it's all in there. Take it but leave me alone."

"Jim you go and check," I said.

Jim raced downstairs and went behind the counter as Heinrich had not yet returned. He found a cardboard box, opened it and found thousands of Euros stuffed in it. He closed the box again and brought it back upstairs.

"It's all here, I think," he said.

"So what now?" I asked quietly.

"We get out of here," replied Jim. "Where's Chad?"

"He was busy keeping the other guy busy so I could get up here."

"Find him and let's get out of here."

I ran down stairs and as I reached the bottom of the stairs, Chad and Heinrich appeared, both looking extremely content.

"And that satisfied look on your face?" I asked.

"I'll tell you later. Did you find them?"

"Yeah and we've got to get out of here quickly. Go and get dressed then I'll join you."

Chad moved off to the lockers while I chattered to Heinrich. Jim in the meantime looked down from the loft and saw me busy talking to Heinrich so he sneaked down the stairs and also went to the lockers to get dressed. I continued talking to Heinrich who informed me that my friend was, and I quote, 'the best fuck' he'd ever had and he had fucked some men in his short life.

"Are you a hustler?" I asked,

"Sure. The guys here know how I can use my dick and they crave it, so I'm always busy and it's always hard. You wanna feel?"

Before I had a chance to touch him up, he grabbed my hand and placed it on his hard crotch. The guy was telling the truth. I could feel his hard cock and my eyes widened as I traced the length of it.

Up stairs, Wellington was still busy with the skinhead. He picked up his jockstrap and stuffed it into the skinhead's mouth, then stood over him looking down at the squirming youth.

"I have two things to say to you," said Wellington, severely, "if you go to the police about this, you're dead and second, if you follow us, I'll have the police onto you on the grounds of trying to exploit tourists."

The skinhead looked at Wellington in a bewildered way.

"Do you understand?" shouted Wellington above the music that was still blaring downstairs.

The skinhead nodded his head as he continued to writhe on the floor.

I then saw Wellington descend the stairs but not go to the lockers to get dressed. Then I noticed something out of the ordinary. He was naked.

"Where's you jockstrap?" I asked when he reached me.

"My friend's chewing on it and thoroughly enjoying it. Why don't you go and get dressed."

Heinrich looked down at Wellington's massive cock and then felt his own.

"That's some dick you've got there, hey?" said the young barman.

Wellington merely smiled.

"Now listen to me and listen carefully. You never saw us tonight, it was all a dream. Your friend upstairs asked that I tell you not to disturb him because he's nursing his ass," said Wellington, holding his cock up for Heinrich to see. "This has been working overtime on him and he's a little in agony, I'm sure you'd understand if you had something this size rammed in your ass."

"Sure," replied Heinrich.

Wellington turned and walked casually to the lockers where he pulled on his clothes, we emptied the cardboard box of its content and stuffed the money into our pockets and even in our briefs and all caught the first train back to the hotel, without a person saying a single word.

11

WHAT NEXT?

When we arrived back at the hotel, we rushed up to Jim and Wellington's room to pack the money away.

"What the hell were you two doing?" I asked when the door to their room was firmly closed. "Both of you sit down and spill the beans. The least you can do is tell Chad and me the truth, after all, we put our lives on the line for you two."

They sensed that I was angry. Jim was the first to speak up.

"Mike, I'm sorry you had to find out like this, but I think I speak on behalf of Wellington as well, when I saw we are grateful to you and Chad for coming to our assistance tonight."

Chad and I stood next to each other and looked down at the two grown men sitting on the bed like two naughty schoolboys.

"It's just that Wellington and I thought we could make some money by selling the uncut diamonds, that's all."

"You know that's not entirely the truth, Jim. If you're going to lie to us, I really don't want to be associated with an uncle who lies, and I'll go so far as to make sure that the whole family knows about you."

The expression on Jim's face was one of self-sorrow.

"I think that this is what you do to make your money, isn't it?" I continued, "Except this time it backfired and you nearly lost your lives through carelessness."

"I know Mike, and I'm truly sorry, but before we go any further, where are the diamonds?"

I unzipped my jeans, dropped them to the floor and stood in my studded jockstrap, then very carefully I popped one of the studs and an uncut diamond fell into my hand.

"You had them on you all the time!" said an exasperated Jim.

Even Wellington had a broad smile on his face when he saw the jockstrap and realized that the diamonds were safe.

"I could hug you and kiss you," said Jim, rising from the bed.

"Sit!" I commanded, "I'm not finished."

Jim sat once more.

"Now tell the truth from the beginning."

Jim cleared his throat and then started.

"Well you know about Wellington and me, obviously? When we met, Wellington had very little money and I had made a fair amount of money from business transactions, then Wellington came up with the idea that we start trading in something, anything, around Europe. I realized that to make money we had to trade in something that would bring in large sums of cash, and we decided that drugs would be too risky."

"And dealing in illicit diamonds is not risky?" I asked.

"Of course it is, but not quite the same as drugs. Any rate, we decided it might be easier to deal in diamonds and so I started visiting Amsterdam and Antwerp to get diamonds."

"And what was Wellington's role in all this?"

"Well, he had various roles. He had a number of contacts in the, let's just say, the 'underworld' so to speak, and I had contacts in the business world. There was, of course another reason for Wellington being used."

"And that was?"

"There were times when I had to win over a buyer and I knew that the potential buyer would enjoy Wellington, if you know what I mean."

"So Wellington would sleep with the buyer, is that it?"

"Yes. But he was very good, because many came back for more and each time we would get the money for the goods."

"So where did all this take place?"

"You mean Wellington's escapades?"

"Yes."

"Those were mainly in London when buyers came to the city, but there were a few times we traveled overseas."

"So what happened tonight?"

"We had arranged to meet the buyer…"

"…the buyer being that skinheads, I presume?"

"Yes. Well, we were going to meet him tonight and hand over the gems in exchange for the money."

"So if you had met in any other place, other than a club that has an underwear only party, you would have been successful?" I asked.

"Probably. The problem was when we got there and he asked for the diamonds; Wellington tried to undo the studs and they wouldn't come off, then we realized he was wearing the wrong jockstrap."

"So you could both have lost your lives because of a jockstrap!" I glared at them. "Is that all your life is worth? And another thing; why couldn't you have put your trust in me and at least told me where you were going?"

"But you found us, thankfully," intervened Wellington.

"Only because when I accidentally popped one of the studs and Chad and I saw the diamond, then we realized what was going on and I remembered you getting a note from the receptionist so I got into your room, found the note and went down to ask the receptionist where the place was. Once he had told us, we caught the underground train and went to the club. As we' didn't know where you guys were, we played dumb and the barman showed us around so that we could get an idea of the layout of the place."

"And Chad throughout all this?" asked Jim.

"I think we all owe Chad a big thank you. He put his ass on the line," I said, proudly.

Wellington and Jim grinned.

"I'm serious. While I was trying to find you, Chad had to get rid of the only other look-out we could see: the barman."

"And how did you do that?" enquired Jim.

Chad blushed profusely and grinned to himself.

"I have an idea that somebody had their ass warmed?" I suggested.

"You mean you had a spanking?" asked Wellington.

"No," replied Chad.

"I spoke to Heinrich, the barman afterwards and he said that Chad was the best fuck he'd ever had."

"Oh wow," echoed Jim and Wellington simultaneously.

"So did you lay into him?" asked Jim.

"No, he had my ass," replied Chad.

"Must be some ass for someone to say you were the best they'd ever had," chimed in Wellington.

"And what's more, Heinrich admitted to me that he was a hustler so he was always screwing guys," I continued proudly. But, tell me, what happens now?"

"Well, I suppose we have a couple of plans," said Jim, reassessing the situation.

"Like what, Jim?" I resumed.

"We could still try to sell the diamonds, or we could hand them over to the police and say we found them and hope they might give us some financial reward, although they haven't been stolen from anywhere. On the other hand, we could keep them."

"And do what with them?" I enquired.

"I don't know. Keep them for a rainy day when we might need to sell them."

"What if those guys from the club come here" asked Chad, "looking for their money and tell the police that we stole it?"

"True, I never thought of that," replied Jim. "Maybe we'd better get out of here."

"And go where?" I asked.

"I do have another contact we could try, if you still want to get rid of the diamonds," suggested Wellington.

"Who and where?" asked Jim.

Wellington hesitated before answering.

"It's OK to say it in front of the boys; after all they saved our asses for us."

"There's a guy in Cologne, here in Germany, who would buy them," answered Wellington.

"Phone him and find out," said Jim, showing more enthusiasm now that there was a possible way out.

"And in the meantime, what do you want me to do with the jockstrap, Jim?" I asked.

"I think you'd better keep it, but somewhere safe."

"Like on his body," quipped Chad. "It looks sexy there."

"Right you guys go to your room and I would suggest you pack your bags in case we have to leave early tomorrow for Cologne, while Wellington and I try to sort pout this problem; but I'll let you know as soon as Wellington has an answer."

Jim opened the bedroom door and Chad and I made our way back to our room.

When we returned to our room, I put my arms around him and hugged him warmly.

"Thank you so much for what you did tonight. I really appreciate it and I know that Jim does as well. You also know what this means?"

"No, what?"

"You're one of the family now. You're part of the team of rogues, if you want to call it that."

"I like the idea of being part of your family, but the rogues bit worries me somewhat."

"Well, then let's just say we're the juniors of the rogues; the decoys; the guys who distract the crooks with out good looks and stunning bodies."

Chad roared with laughter at my descriptions.

"You know, you joke about it, but who knows, we might have been killed or at the least, locked up in jail fro smuggling. Did you think of that?"

"The only things that I thought of were your s, Jims and Wellington's safety."

"Why mine?"

"Well, I'd left you with Heinrich and as I didn't know him, he could have done anything to you."

"Put like that, he did do something to me."

"So tell me, how come you were the best fuck he'd ever had? What did you do that you've never done with me?"

"It wasn't what I did; it was what he did and it turned me on."

"Why what did he do to you?"

When he had come and emptied his load into me I thought it was all over, but no, he pulled out and holding his stiff cock, which was quite a size, he played with the entrance to my asshole."

"How do you mean?"

"Well with his cock head he pushed just the head back into my ass and then pulled out, teasingly. Then he repeated this over and over, pushing the head in and pulling it out and each time my ass clamped tight around it. It felt as if he did this for hours, but the pleasure we both got from it was amazing. I actually just wanted him to sink his cock back into my chute and fuck me all over again."

"Well then, maybe I must try that and see what happens," I answered with a devilish grin on my face.

Our erotic conversation was cut short by the shrill ringing of the telephone. I picked up the receiver and heard Jim's voice on the other end.

"Mike, we're leaving for Cologne on the 9:00a.m train tomorrow. I've made accommodation arrangement for Cologne and told the reception that we'll be booking out early tomorrow. Wear your jockstrap tomorrow so that I know the diamonds are safe, and pack your bags if you haven't already done so. Good night, kid and thanks again."

"G' night, Jim."

I replaced the receive and smiled to Chad.

"We're off to Cologne tomorrow morning, honey, so pack those bags and let's get some sleep."

12

COLOGNE

Our train left Berlin heading for Leipzig and then on to Cologne. We settled in for the long journey, all feeling more relaxed at having left Berlin behind, although we had no issues with the city and its people. The countryside flashed by and we contended ourselves by reminiscing our fun time in Berlin.

"So tell us about this wonderful time you had while Jim and I were almost at death's door," asked Wellington.

"I don't think Chad wants to give all the juicy detail, Wellington, suffice to say he was good at what he did," I said, hoping to change the topic because it was worrying me that I might not be able to perform the way that Heinrich had pleased Chad. "Jim, what are you r plans once we get to Cologne?"

"Book ourselves into our hotel, relax and wait for Wellington to make contact with the guy. He has already phoned and told him we were leaving this morning, so nothing will take place at least until maybe two day's time."

"So long?" I queried.

"Tomorrow we'll probably just find our bearings as I've never been to Cologne before, but I hear it's quite an interesting place."

"The only thing I know about it," said Chad, "is that it's got an amazing Gothic cathedral and it's a very old city. Do you know anything about it, Mike?"

"I remember reading once that it had quite a good leather scene. I think most of the bars and the leather scene are centered near the cathedral."

"Oh so you can have your fun and sex, and then nip into the cathedral and confess your sins. Is that how it works?" asked Jim.

"I wouldn't think it was quite that bad," I responded, "but at least it seems to be a fun-filled city, and when I say fun-filled, I don't mean dodging crooks or running away from the police."

Wellington sat dozing off to sleep and the constant gentle rocking of the train as it flashed past the countryside, was soon having a similar effect on all of us. Within minutes, Jim was snoring his head off while Chad rested his head on my shoulder.

"Are you awake?" I whispered into Chad's ear.

He raised his head and smiled at me, then replaced his head on my shoulder. It felt so good to feel his warmth resting on me.

"Chad, do you really have feelings for me?" I continued in a whisper so as not to wake Wellington or Jim.

"Of course I do," came the reply. "Do you like me?"

"No," I whispered back.

Chad's head shot up and he glared at me. I pushed his head back onto my shoulder.

"I hadn't finished. No, I don't like you...I love you," I said quietly.

He squeezed my thigh and smiled to himself.

"Do you really?" he asked, not looking at me.

"Of course I do. I've realized what a great influence you have over me and I know this might sound stupid to you, but I reckon I could spend the rest of my life with you."

There was no reaction from Chad for a moment, and then he lifted his head once more, turned to face me and kissed me passionately on the lips.

"I'd like that," he said, when our lips parted. "What do you feel?"

"I think I'm falling more and more in love with you as well. I think I realized that when we were in that club in Berlin. I was genuinely worried about you and I know you said you had a good time with Heinrich, but I have to admit it, I was jealous."

"Jealous of what?"

"At first I was jealous that he'd be having sex with you, but I realized that it was part of the plan, and then when you both said you had the best sex, I began to think that maybe I was inadequate."

"Mike, you're far from being inadequate. You're a beautiful lover and I really do like having sex with you. Sorry, I lie. I like it when you make love to me. Having sex is emotionless to me, but making love brings out all the passion you have in you. Sure, the way Heinrich used his cock was awesome and it did bring a feeling of excitement, but it was short-lived. You must remember it was only the end part that was exciting. With you, from the time we start kissing and fondling each other to the time we come, it's exciting, so please don't ever think you're inadequate."

I leaned over and kissed the top of his head and felt him squeeze my thigh again.

"Can we make love tonight when we get to Cologne?"

"Of course, I would expect it and if you're a good guy, I might even slip my cock into you and teach you a thing or two."

I gave a little snigger at Chad's suggestion, but I didn't put it out of my mind; I would like him to make love to me. Jim had penetrated me back in London and I had enjoyed it, so why wouldn't I let the man who I was falling in love with do the same to me?

"You might just get lucky," I whispered into his ear, and felt the squeeze once more.

The only sounds that emanated after that were the clicking of the trains' wheels on the railway line and Jim and Wellington's snoring. Chad had fallen asleep and I held him in my arms, cradling his head and caressing his hair.

After a very long journey, our train pulled into the Köln or Cologne, as we called it, Haupbahnhof or main railway station. We rose and stretched out tired bodies, then alighted and looked for a cab.

"There's the cathedral," said Chad, pointing excitedly in the direction of the twin spires.

"Where's our hotel, Jim?" I asked once we had exited the station.

He pulled out a slip of paper on which he'd written all the details and read it.

"The hotel's in a street by the name of Hohe Pfoerte, if I've written it down correctly and apparently there are a number of clubs in the vicinity, especially one in Mathiasstrasse," said Jim.

"Why what's so special about that club?" I asked.

"My source says we must look for a red door and behind it we'll find such exciting things as a cage, in which you can keep Mike prisoner, Chad; there are cruising areas, a darkroom and a sling room, so you can take your pick for your fun."

"Are they open every, Jim?" enquired Wellington.

"You see, he's getting excited already. As far as I know, yes they are, and apparently on Sundays, you boys could let it all hang out – it's naked day."

"Oh wow!" exclaimed Chad.

"Let's hope we stay that long," I remarked.

A cab finally came along and we all bundled in and made our way to our hotel, which proved to be not that far from the railway station. While we booked into two rooms, as usual, Wellington made a phone call to the contact, telling him that we had arrived in Cologne. As it was late already, Jim had been right in estimating that the meeting between Jim and Wellington with the contact would take place in two day's time, it meant we had time to kill and have a look around the city and check out its men; our favorite pastime.

"Do you guys feel like going out tonight?" enquired Jim.

"I'm ready to party," I said, "What about you, Chad?"

"Can't wait to hit the town; and you Wellington, are you raring to go?"

"I don't need much persuasion," he answered.

"So what's it going to be?" asked Jim, hoping that one of us younger guys would make the decision for him.

"Well, I don't know about you guys, but I haven't worn my new rubber outfit properly, so I reckon we should hit one of those leather clubs you said were round here somewhere/"

"Sounds good to me," commented Wellington, "especially after what I went through in Berlin, I think I need some stimulation."

"Don't I stimulate you enough?" questioned Jim.

"Of course you do, James, but I need to break loose for a bit."

Chad and I glanced at each other on hearing Wellington say 'break loose' and wondered just how wild he got when he did break loose.

"I think we should go and have something to eat and then go in search of a club," suggested Jim.

So the four of us wandered the streets to find a restaurant to have something to eat. The sight was one of wonder to the many Germans who passed us. The reason they all looked and stared was because of Wellington's height and build. The rest of us looked like midgets next to him and his striking facial features were also outstanding.

The food we had was, to say the least, adequate although it was plentiful. Along with our meal which included sauerkraut, which Wellington found distasteful, we ordered four glasses of great German beer. The one thing I will say about the Germans is that they now how to make beer and personally, I also think they produce good-looking men, that is, with the exception of Chad.

After having something to fill our stomachs, we made our way back to the hotel to get changed for our night out.

"Mike, do you think I could borrow your chaps if you're not wearing them," Chad asked.

"Sure, no problem, because I'm going to wear my rubber outfit with the kinky zip, especially for you," I said with a twinkle in my eyes. "But what are you going to wear with the chaps?"

"My new jockstrap, the one with the front zip."

"Great, then you will be able to get access to my deliciously tight ass," I jokingly said to Chad.

In the other room, Wellington was preparing himself for a striking evening. His bald head glistened in the hotel room light as he put on his leather harness with a cock ring attachment, like Chad's. Then he pulled on a pair of chaps and zipped them up, encasing his muscular legs with the tight material. Jim, on the other hand, was playing it safe. Although he was dressed in leather as well, he was going in his jeans and a leather shirt, boots and soft leather gloves. Once we were all dressed, we met in the foyer of the hotel reception area. There were obvious the stares of tourist who were also staying at the same hotel, but their stares didn't perturb us.

"You're looking extremely sexy tonight, Duke," I said walking around him to observe him from all angles.

"Why, thank you kind sir," he replied in jovial mood.

"And what about me?" asked Jim, "Don't I com up to scratch?"

"Of course you do," answered Chad. "You always look sexy no matter what you wear."

"Hey, are you trying to flirt with my uncle?" I teasingly asked.

"I'll flirt with whomever I like," retorted Chad, giving my ass a light slap.

"Hey, mind the ass, that's reserved."

"Who for?" questioned Chad.

"For a very hunky man who I hope will make a pass at me tonight and maybe whip me off to bed with him."

"I don't know about whipping you off to bed, but you might find yourself getting a whipping, that's if there are any whips and chains around," replied Chad.

"I'll help you there," said Wellington, also giving my ass a slap.

"What's with the ass slapping tonight?" I queried.

"We just like you ass, that's all," Chad jested.

We found the red door as was told to us, paid and went in. The atmosphere inside was electric.

"Wow this is some place," I commented on seeing the red lighting, hearing the loud music, thumping and seeing all the leather-clad men.

"Down Fido," said Jim, when he saw me leering at all the men. Remember you've got a very handsome man with you."

"Are you talking about yourself, Jim?"

"No, cheeky; you've got Chad."

"I know. I was just looking. Surely there's no harm in looking?"

We made our way to the bar counter and ordered four beers. We stood there at the counter with our beers, taking in the whole scene.

"You a visitor?" shouted the barman to us over the loud music.

"Yes," I shouted back. "Nice club this."

The barman smiled as a result of his club being complimented.

"Where are you from?"

"I'm from America. He's from Canada," pointing to Chad, "and they're from London."

Our barman can best be described as lofty, strapping and attractive. He was wearing a leather harness and a pair of chaps under which he had on a studded jockstrap like the one that I had back at the hotel.

"Do you get a lot of locals coming in here?" I continued with the conversation.

"Yes most nights. Not only is the music good, but we have ideal, clean facilities. Have you seen our facilities?"

"No, this is our first time here."

"You must wander around and see them."

"I believe you have a sling room, dark room and a couple of other interesting rooms," I added, based on what Jim had told us.

He stretched out a large hand to shake mine,

"I'm Henk," he said shaking my hand with his vice-like grip.

"Hi, there, I'm Mike."

I wondered if I should introduce the others to Henk the hunk, but decided not to.

"Do you wanna dance, Chad?" asked Wellington, and immediately the two of them hit he dance floor. All eyes were on the two handsome men on the dance floor.

"I get a break in half an hour," said Henk to me. Would you like to join me and I'll show you around."

"Sounds good to me," I replied; keen to know where everything was situated in the club.

A middle-aged man in a rubber outfit approached Jim for a dance and he accepted, which left me with Henk at the bar.

"Your friend has a very good body," said Henk, indicating Wellington and Chad, but I wasn't sure which friend he was referring to.

"Which one?" I asked.

"The Black guy."

"Oh yes, he has."

"Those guys are also big, if you get what I mean."

"Oh yes, you can see from his jockstrap that there's quite a bit packed in there."

"I like Black guys. They make good lovers, do you know that?"

"No, I didn't," I said, knowing that my reply was totally stupid. If they didn't make good lovers, why had Jim stayed with Wellington so long?

"Is he your boyfriend?" enquired Henk.

"No. The other guy is."

I suddenly realized what I had said. For the first time I had actually acknowledged that Chad was my boyfriend. I stood silent and stared at Chad. He really was beautiful both physically and with an inner beauty.

"He is also good-looking."

"Yes, he is," I automatically replied without even thinking what I was saying.

The music ended and Wellington and Chad returned to where I was standing to pick up their drinks.

"I think the barman likes you, Duke," I said softly so the barman never heard me.

"Did he say so?" enquired Wellington.

"He said he was very into Black guys, mainly because they have such big dicks."

"I bet he never said anything of the kind."

"Ask him, if you don't believe me. Henk let me introduce you. This is Wellington."

Henk stretched across the bar counter and took Wellington's hand and shook it. Their smiles met and I felt there was an element of chemistry between them. Both were muscular; both were handsome and both looked as horny as hell.

"Henk's going off for a break just now and would like to show you around," I continued.

"Can I do that?" asked Henk when he heard me say that to Wellington.

"Sure, sure."

I took the trouble to lean over the counter to get a look at Henk's equipment and was pleasantly pleased to see a hefty bulge in his jockstrap, so I thought both he and Wellington would make each other happy.

When Henk cam off duty for his break, he and Wellington went down a dark corridor and disappeared.

"Should we follow to see where everything is?" I enquired of Chad.

"Why not," was the reply.

So while Jim amused himself on the dance floor, Chad and I went off to scout out the club, and if possible, see what Wellington and Henk might be up to.

We found a dark room where we floundered around, trying to feel our way in the dark and coming across a number of half naked bodies. However, we stuck together as we didn't want to lose each other and eventually emerged from the darkroom unscathed. We then entered the sling room and saw Wellington and Henk together. Chad and I stood in a darkened corner and watched. There were also a number of other men in the room as well busily preoccupied.

Wellington and Henk's lips were locked together and we could see how they ground their crotches together, getting themselves harder all the time. Wellington then sank to his knees and began to lick Henk's jockstrap in the front, then after he had nibbled at the pouch and wet it thoroughly, he turned Henk around and began to part his ass cheeks. Wellington's tongue went in search of Henk's pucker and soon Henk was bent over while Wellington's tongue gave his asshole a solid washing. We could see how Henk writhed with ecstasy as his ass was targeted by Wellington's mouth. Interspersed with the tongue washing, were nibbles that Wellington administered to Hen's ass cheeks, then Wellington rose once more to his feet and guided Henk towards the vacant sling'. He helped Henk into the sling, hoisted his muscular legs so they rested on the steel chains, then he bent forward and pulled Henk's cock from the confines of his jockstrap and sank his mouth over it until it went to the back of his throat. Wellington's mouth remained glued to the long cock, his chin rubbing against Henk's balls, and then he slid his mouth up to the tip. A long, low growl came from Henk's throat, and Wellington proceeded to take Henk's cock back down his throat again.

I knew my cock was leaking pre-cum from the pleasure they were giving me and I was sure that Chad would be in the same condition. I stretched my hand across to Chad's crotch and felt his rock-hard cock, which was actually protruding from the top of his jockstrap he had become so aroused. I ran my hand over his hard cock and then gripped it. He sighed when did that. I didn't have to unzip his jockstrap as his cock was already sticking well over the top of the waist band, so instead I pushed his jockstrap down to allow his cock total freedom, then I moved in front of him and stood there.

I felt Chad take hold of the zip at the back of my rubber shorts and begin to unzip them, and then I felt his warm hand caress my bare ass. His finger tickled my ass and then slid down my crack as he ventured closer to my pulsating hole. It didn't take Chad long to find it and begin exploring. His finger dug deep into me and began to grind my insides. I pushed back so his finger went even deeper and both of us sighed happily.

In the meantime, Wellington had taken to rimming Henk and salivating over Henk's hole, preparing it for his assault. I watched as Wellington took hold of his thick shaft and guided it towards the pulsating, hole. Slowly he pushed forward, sinking ever so slowly into Henk who was groaning as the thick, bulbous head forced its way into the warm chute.

At the same time I felt Chad's cock head nudge my pucker and then he began his slow entry. I was about to receive my second pleasurable experience. I grunted as I felt Chad's swollen cock push into me, but I never resisted; I wanted him inside of me then we would be one. Slowly

I pushed back to meet his thrust. As I did so, so Chad wrapped his arms around me and rubbed his hands over my rubber encased cock, which was aching to get free. I needed the freedom, so I grabbed the zipper between my legs and unzipped the front. My cock sprung free as Chad sank his cock to the hilt into my ass. Both of us moaned as he hit my prostate and massaged it with his cock head and at the same time He began jacking my cock off; his soft hands sliding effortlessly along my long shaft and massaging my cut head with my pre-cum. The electric sensation as my wet pre-cum made his strokes easier, excited me, then he started to pull out, but I didn't want him to leave, so I clamped my ass muscles as tight as I could manage. Chad groaned even more loudly when I did that.

"Oh fuck, that feels so good, Mike," he whispered in my ear. "You've got the most awesome ass, babes."

His slow, deep thrusts were making me see stars before my eyes and with each thrust it felt as though his cock was growing thicker and harder.

In the sling, Wellington had taken control of their scene and was plowing his cock faster and faster into Henk, who was encouraging him to 'fuck me harder!' Both men were now grunting with each thrust and the sweat was pouring down Wellington's chest, making his body glisten in the available light. The chains of the sling were creaking and it was swaying back and forth with tremendous gusto.

Watching Wellington and Henk was driving both Chad and me closer to our climaxes and I knew that with Chad's grinding in my ass I wasn't going to last much longer.

"Chad you're getting me close," I whispered, but it didn't deter him.

The loud slapping of flesh against flesh echoed around the room as Wellington plugged Henk's tight hole and Chad did the same to me.

"Oh Fuck! I'm gonna shoot," I cried, and immediately a spray of cum ejected from my cock and flew onto the concrete floor.

At he same time my ass muscles clamped tightly around Chad's cock causing him to explode from the excitement. I felt his shots of juice fill my chute making his thrusts even more slippery and smooth inside of me and together we shuddered and groaned, his mouth kissing the back of my neck as each load exited from his throbbing cock.

Wellington and Henk's groans and cries were no different from ours and they two expended their juices to each other.

I felt Chad start to withdraw from me and I whispered to him, "please don't. I want you to stay in me. Keep thrusting. I want to feel you cock hitting my prostate more."

Chad knew what to do. His thrusts were not sharp, but long deep and penetrating and with each those stars that I'd been seeing the whole time reappeared before me and I wanted to go through the whole session again. Then I felt him leave me and a sense of emptiness filled my being, but not for long. Holding the stem of his cock, he slowly pushed the head back into my chute and quickly pulled out again. He repeated this time and time again, driving me wild with passion until I couldn't take it any longer and pushed back onto him, impaling my ass on his cock.

"Fuck me again babes," I cried, grinding my ass on his cock.

Wellington and Henk kissed and got out of the sling, stood facing each other and hugged; their cocks still hard, rubbing together, and then left the room.

Without removing his cock from me, Chad and I moved over to the sling which was still warm from Henk's body and for the first time, Chad slid out of me as he helped me into the sling and then sank his beautiful long, thick cock back into my warm chute and we continued making love together.

While I lay with my legs hoisted and spread well apart, Chad gave me a rollercoaster ride of orgasmic pleasure, bringing me to highs and then letting me down gently only to rise me to another high. His build-ups were driving my body to spasms of joy and all I wanted to do was for us to shoot our load and for him to fill me again.

When we had finally and exhaustedly left the sling room, we got back to the bar counter to find Wellington and Henk deep in conversation. We ordered a beer each and as he sat, both in a surreal, yet fantastic state of elation, Jim arrived from the dance floor with his middle-aged friend.

"I've got the exact location of where we have to go," said Jim excitedly.

"Jim," interrupted Wellington.

"We can take the goods there and it's within easy walking distance."

"Jim!" repeated Wellington.

"Maybe we should leave them in the jockstrap,"

"JIM!" exploded Wellington.

"What's your problem?"

"Jim, just shut up for a minute. Have you looked carefully at Henk?" asked Wellington, now getting frustrated.

"No, why?" asked Jim, taking a good look at Henk.

"He's Heinz's brother," said Wellington, with an artificial smile on his face.

"You mean, Heinz the cop?"

"The very same."

Jim gave a nervous laugh.

"Oh, how nice," he replied, blushing as he did so.

"Wellington told me how my brother saved his ass when you guys arrived in Berlin."

"Yes… yes," replied the highly embarrassed Jim. "He was very good to us."

"Where did you know him from?" enquired Henk.

"We met in Amsterdam at their Leather Pride," continued Jim.

Just then Jim's dance partner spoke up unexpectedly.

"You want me to take you to this place tomorrow?"

"NO!" Shouted Jim, more out of embarrassment. "No, thanks."

The little middle-aged man took umbrage at being shouted at and decided to take himself off to meet someone else.

"Was there somewhere you wanted to go?" asked Henk.

"No, we know were to go?" replied Jim.

"Henk tells me he's totally different from his brother," said Wellington, trying to change the subject.

"Oh really, in what way?" asked Jim.

"He's the good one and I'm the naughty one," said Henk with a glint in his eye.

"Naughty in what way?" asked Wellington.

"Not the way you think. We both like men, but I was naughty in other ways."

"You know, something that's fascinated me," I said, joining in the conversation, "did you and he ever have sex together? I think it's kinky when brothers do it together."

Henk laughed.

"All the time. If he went out and didn't pick up anyone, he would always come home and plow his dick into my ass. It's actually great having it off with your brother because you have a different relationship with each other and there's a loving, caring side to it."

"What sort of naughty things did you do?" asked Jim.

"I used to do drugs fro a while and I used to steal the odd thing to get money to buy the drugs."

"Do you still do drugs, Henk?" I asked, my mind beginning to plot things out.

"Sometimes, when I've got a bit of extra cash."

"Jim," I said, turning to him. "I think I need to go to the toilet, won't you come with me please?"

"What on earth for? Do you want me to hold your cock while you piss?"

I gave him a stony look and nodded my head towards the direction of the toilet.

"OK, but let's make it quick," replied Jim.

We made our way to the toilet while Wellington and Chad kept Henk busy. When we entered there were a couple of guys busy at the urinal, while others were busy in one of the corners. I took Jim to a cubicle and stood in the doorway.

"Jim, why don't we get Henk involved in our deal?"

"Our deal? I told you this is between Wellington and me. I'm not getting you and Chad involved."

"Listen to me. If Henk's involved and if anything untoward happens, he's got a cop as a brother who might get him off. In fact if they have such a close bond that they're happily having sex together, it means his brother would do anything for him."

"I don't know Mike. It could be a bit risky involving him."

"Sure, I understand, but I'm thinking of you and I don't want you to get into trouble again, especially if you don't want Chad or I involved."

"But why involve him in the first place?"

"He wants money and I'm sure you could give him a cut of the takings."

"But why?"

"OK, here's another plan. Why not sell the diamonds to Henk and he can do with them what he likes?"

"Because I don't think he'd have the finances to pay for them."

"Point taken."

"Mike, leave things as they are. The fewer people who are involved, the better."

"Fine, but I still worry about you and Wellington."

"I know you do, and I respect that, so let's get back to them otherwise they'll think we're occupied with each other."

We made our way back to the bar counter and pretended that nothing untoward had been discussed. We had a few more drinks with Henk and then the four of us made our way back to our hotel, but not before Wellington had made another date with Henk.

The following day was spent taking in the sights of Cologne and taking a walk to the spot where we were to meet the contact.

"I'm glad you never told the contact where we were staying, Wellington," said Jim, "otherwise we'd be on the run again if things went wrong."

We wandered down towards the Rhine River and spotted the cruise boat on which Jim and Wellington had arranged to meet their contact the following day.

"What time are you guys meeting him?" I asked.

"At 6:00p.m," replied Wellington.

There was a moment of silence as I pondered the idea of being around when they did the transaction. I still thought about Henk and if he would become involved. I even wondered if I should tell him and ask him to contact his brother, Heinz, so the police could apprehend the contact, but then I wondered if they'd also apprehend Jim and Wellington. My concerns for Jim and Wellington's safety were worrying me, so I took Chad aside as spoke to him.

"Chad, I'm worried about the meeting that Jim and Wellington are planning."

"What aspect's worrying you, Mike?"

"It's their safety. They've already had one close call and I don't want a second. I was wondering if we should tell Henk about what's planned so that he could phone his brother who might contact the police here and they could apprehend the contact."

"That could be a bit risky, don't you think?"

"Personally, I'd like to take those damn diamonds and throw them away."

"I know how you feel, because I'd feel the same way," said Chad, putting an arm around my shoulder. "But leave them to do their own thing."

I realized that both Wellington and Jim had made up their minds to go through with the transaction and nothing would change their minds, so I resigned myself to the rest of the day's sightseeing.

"You know what I'd like to see," said Chad, "is the inside of the cathedral. Would you join me, Mike?"

"Of course. Hey you guys, we're going to the cathedral if you want to join us."

Jim and Wellington decided that they didn't want heavenly intervention and turned down the offer, so Chad and I headed off to Roncalliplatz where we passed the Römisch-Germanisches Museum and reached the Dom. We entered and were knocked out by the beauty of its interior. It can only be described as splendorous and enormous and as we made our way closer to the High Altar, we were taken by the magnificence of the altar slab and backdrop. Chad then moved to the Gothic stalls and sat down in one of them. I went and sat down beside him in the quiet of the building, while the rest of the world rushed frenetically outside.

"Are you a religious person, Chad?"

"Not really, but when you encounter something like this, it makes you think."

I sat back and looked up at the high ceilings and considered how it was built so many hundreds of years ago and then thought of how simple we had actually become in our modern lives.

In the silence, it allowed us both to ponder on our lives and what was happening to us. I stretched my hand along the oak seat and touched Chad's leg. His hand came to meet mine and we clasped hands. I felt his gentle squeeze, so I reciprocated, then we turned to each other and our eyes met. I could see the love in his face and I knew he could see my feelings for him.

"Chad, I feel I have to do something," I whispered.

"What? Are you going to kiss me here in the cathedral in front of these people?"

"No, but that's not a bad idea. I was considering asking Henk to contact his brother to see if we could stop this transaction tomorrow night somehow."

Chad never said a word, but continued to look into my eyes.

"That's also why I love you Mike; your truth and honesty as well as your concern for those in your life. Shall we go and see if we could find Henk?"

My smile must have spread from ear to ear when I heard Chad say that. Taking him by the hand, I dragged him out of the cathedral and went in search of Henk.

When we arrived at the club we found it closed, but a cleaner said that Henk was inside, cleaning up from the previous night.

"Could we get in to see him, please?" I asked.

The cleaner obliged and we went into the stale smoke-smelling club. It looked different without the glitz of the lighting or the sound of the vibrant music, but we found Henk busy behind the bar counter.

"Henk, we're so sorry to worry you..."

"Mike, what are you guys doing here, we're not open."

"We know that, but we had to see you and talk to you."

"You sound serious has something happened to Wellington?"

"No, Henk, he's fine, at the moment. But it does concern him."

What's happened. Sit down. Can I get you guys something to drink?"

"No, nothing for us thanks. We have to talk to you, but they don't know that we're doing this."

I hesitated, not knowing quite how to explain everything to Henk.

"First let me say that both Wellington and Jim are actually wonderful people, and your brother Heinz actually took a liking to Jim. Well ... they might be getting themselves into trouble..."

Henk laughed.

"I don't think either could get into trouble."

"Uhm... you see they have a package which they are selling to someone tomorrow evening... and I don't want them to get into trouble..."

"Is it something illegal, like drugs?" asked Henk, his eyes lighting up a little.

"You could say that, but it's not drugs."

"So what do you want me to do?"

I was hoping you could contact your brother and tell him what was going to go down and maybe he could contact the local [police and apprehend the contact, but not Wellington or Jim."

"We know we're asking a helluva lot from you, Henk, but it's only because we feel for the two guys," said Chad, pleadingly.

"So what musty I tell Heinz?" asked Henk.

"They've got a package. But I don't know yet what form it will take, and they're meeting the contact at 6:00p.m on a cruise boat on the Rhine."

"What's in the package?"

"Diamonds. Uncut ones."

"Let me phone Heimz now before you go and see what he says."

Henk picked up the phone and dialed his brother's number. When his brother answered, their conversation was conducted entirely in German. There were one or two words that I recognized, but other than that, I had not idea what he was telling him. When he had completed his conversation he replaced the telephone and smiled at both of us.

"All is well. Heinz will sort it out for you."

"But Wellington and Jim will be safe. I mean they're not going to arrest them are they?"

"I explained everything you told me. Do you know who the contact is?"

I shook my head.

"No idea at all."

"Heinz was very pleased to hear that you guys were here and he's decided that he's going to fly to Köln to deal with the transaction himself. I think he'd like to see Jim again."

"When is he coming?"

"Today or maybe tonight, but he said he'd like to speak to Jim and find out more details."

"Thanks Henk, I owe you big time," I said, happy to know that something was going to be done.

"Come round tonight and I'll get payment for what you owe me," joked Henk, "that's if Chad allows me."

"Why do you say that Henk?" asked Chad.

"I saw you last night. While I was lying in the sling, I watched you two guys and that turned me on even more."

"We didn't know you saw us," I said, "but I can assure you it was you and Wellington who turned us on."

"Also Heinz will probably be here tonight so he can speak to Jim."

"Thanks again, Henk, we really are grateful to you."

Chad and I left the club and went out into the bright sunlit street, happier in our hearts.

"What do you think Jim's going to say when we tell him, Mike?"

"Oh probably kill us both, I should imagine."

"Seriously, do you think he's going to be angry?"

"To be honest, he might, but I think once he realizes that we're doing it for his own good, he might have a change of heart."

13

A LITTLE HELP
FROM YOUR FRIENDS

Back at the hotel, neither Chad nor I said anything to Jim or Wellington when we saw them about our visit to Henk or the telephone call made to Berlin. Instead we spoke only about going to the club that evening.

"Are you wearing the same as last night, Mike?" asked Chad.

"Why, are you planning to have my ass again?"

"No, it's just that I wondered if we'd spend more time discussing the plan with Heinz than visiting the various rooms."

"I see what you mean. You've got a point there. Maybe I'll wear my denim jeans," I answered. "What about you, babes?"

"I haven't given it much thought, but maybe I'll do the same as you. By the way, just off the topic of clothing, have you got the jockstrap with the diamonds?"

I went to our cupboard where I'd put our clothes and found the jockstrap.

"Yeah, it's here."

"Maybe you should wear it tonight in case Heinz wants to see that we really do have the diamonds."

"Good idea."

Again, the four of us went out to dinner that evening and after that, we all went to the club without Jim or Wellington aware of who was going to be there.

When we arrived, I rushed up to Henk and told him not to say a word to either Jim or Wellington, as we hadn't told them of our plan. We ordered some beers each and sat listening to the music. We were earlier than usual, so the club was less crowded but it still had a number of horny guys in leather preening themselves and eyeing each other.

"Where's Heinz?" I whispered to Henk.

"I reckon he should be here within half an hour."

"I don't know about you guys, but I think I'm going to wander around a bit," said Jim, heading off in the direction of the sling room.

Wellington and Henk got busy chatting to each other and so I asked Chad if he wanted to wander around a bit.

"I think I'll just sit here for a while," he replied.

"Do you mind if I go for a walk?" I asked.

"Not at all, you go for it."

I headed off in the same direction that Jim had taken and came across the cage in which a naked young man was lying on the mattress in the cage. When he saw me, he scrambled to the edge of the cage and extended his arm out to me. I neared him and he ran his hand over my crotch, feeling my flaccid cock, then he quickly unzipped my jeans, pulled on my jockstrap and pulled my cock out where he proceeded to suck on it trying to get it hard. As I wasn't being turned on by him, I pulled away, zipped up and headed on. I entered the cruising darkroom area and had to wait as my eyes adjusted to the limited light. When I felt I was ready I slowly walked into the area. I could see figures huddled together, some completely naked and others just with their zips undone. On one side I noticed two young men on their knees and Jim between them. The one had his mouth plugged to Jim's cock while the other was giving Jim's ass a tongue washing. After a while the guy working on Jim's ass moved to the front and both young men started licking and sucking on Jim's fully erect cock. Watching this was a turn on for me and I felt my cock standing erect in my jockstrap. I wondered if I should join Jim, but decided that he had left alone, so he probably didn't want another person there from our party, so I moved on. From there I went into the sling room. The only person there was a guy about my age, lying naked in the sling obviously waiting for someone, anyone to come and attack his ass. He lay there fully erect, playing with his cock, stroking it ever so slowly, with his legs raised and his pucker waiting to be invaded. I walked over to him and let my fingers slide over his asshole. He opened his eyes from his trance and smiled up at me.

He said, "Fick mich!"

I didn't understand so I continued running my fingers down his ass crack and teasing his hole.

"Oo ja, fick mich!"

He brought his hand down to his ass and inserted two fingers into his asshole. I wondered if that was what he wanted me to do, so I inserted two of my fingers in alongside his. His ass opened wider and I felt his warmth as my fingers sank in.

"Blase mir einen!" he said.

I still didn't understand, but instinct kicked in. Keeping my fingers embedded in his ass and twisting them in his ass, I leaned over and wrapped my mouth around his young, hard cock that was oozing pre-cum pretty furiously. I tasted his sweet-saltiness and sank my mouth till my chin hit his stomach. He lay cooing quietly as my fingers and my mouth worked him over. Very soon his cooing turned to gasping and a flood of young German semen shot into my mouth. I swallowed and ground my fingers deeper into his ass, causing him to writhe with each blast from his cock. After a couple of mouthfuls, I released my grip on his cock and watched as the remnants slid down the shaft of his cock, then I licked up the length of his shaft, taking his leftovers into my throat. When I knew that his cock was dry of juices, I slowly withdrew my fingers from his pulsating ass.

"Danke," he said and smiled up at me again.

I wandered on through various rooms and then headed to the toilet for a piss. As I unzipped and pulled out my semi hard cock from my jockstrap, Henk walked into the toilet.

"Heinz is here," he said, unzipping his jeans and pulling out his cock.

Instinctively we both looked down at each other's cock.

"You had some fun?" asked Henk, looking down at my cock.

"No, giving someone fun," I replied.

I looked at his long cock and admired its shape and size. The more I looked at it, the harder mine became and I was finding it hard to piss. Henk noticed how my cock was growing in length and girth and he stroked his cock to get it harder. I couldn't prevent myself, but as soon as my cock was standing like a periscope on a German U-boat, I started stroking myself. Henk stretched a hand across and took hold of my rock hard erection.

"You have a beautiful cock, Mike."

"Thanks, yours is also awesome," I returned the compliment, and I meant it.

I didn't bother to wrap my hands around his shaft, instead I san k to my knees at the urinal and engulfed his engorged cock into my throat. I didn't care who came into the toilet and saw us. I sucked for a while then he pulled me to my feet and sank to his knees. I knew I wouldn't last long having been through the pleasure of the guy in the sling and now Henk.

"Henk I'm coming!" I groaned.

He released his mouth and jacked me off until I shot onto his face. My cum sprayed across his cheeks and his forehead. When my firing had subsided, he licked the remaining cum from the tip of my cock, still jacking me as he did so, then he stood up and pushed his cock back into his jeans and zipped up

"What about you?" I asked.

"I've got the whole night still," he smiled. "Come, let's go and see Heinz."

We left the toilet and went back to the bar. When we arrived there, Jim had also appeared and was very surprised at seeing Heinz.

"What are you doing here?" asked Jim, looking at me with suspicion.

"I think we need to talk, Jim," said Heinz. "Henk is there somewhere we can go and talk in private?"

Henk offered us the club's private office and so the four of us plus Heinz squeezed into the tiny room.

"Now Jim, I want the truth about what's going on."

"I don't know what you're talking about Heinz."

"Please don't lie to me; I know that you're up to something."

"Is this your doing Mike?" asked Jim with an element of venom in his voice.

"Jim, you can hate me for the rest of your life, but because I love you as an Uncle, I don't want you getting into trouble again, so yes, it was my idea of calling on Heinz to help. If you're not happy with me, then I'm sorry and you won't ever have to deal with me again, but I want an uncle who I can trust, someone I can be proud of and not someone who's sitting behind prison bars. This also goes for you too Wellington. Chad and I spoke long and hard about this and it was a joint decision to try and save you both."

Both Wellington and Jim sat quietly listening.

"So now do you want to tell me what's happening?" enquired Heinz.

Jim found that he couldn't bring himself to say anything and remained quiet. Wellington just stood dumbstruck.

"Wellington, I agreed to help Chad and Mike because I like you and didn't want you to get into trouble either," said Henk. "I know that you and Jim are in a partnership, but that still doesn't mean I can't have feeling for you and when the guys told me, I immediately became worried that you might get hurt."

Again Wellington couldn't say anything.

"Mike, would you like to tell me what's going on if they're not able to?" enquired Heinz.

I decided not to tell Heinz the whole story, but only what was planned for Cologne.

"Jim and Wellington came into some uncut diamonds and decided to sell them, so Wellington said he had a contact here who might buy them and the two were going to meet with the person tomorrow evening and sell them to him."

"So where are the diamonds now?"

"I've go them."

"Where? Are they at your hotel?"

I grinned.

"No. I've got them on me now."

"Let me see them," Asked Heinz.

I looked apprehensively at the others and then kicked off my shoes, unzipped my jeans and stepped out of them. I stood in the small office-like room in my studded jockstrap.

"And this?" enquired Heinz.

I then carefully popped one of the studs and out fell an uncut diamond which I handed to Heinz. He smiled broadly at me.

"I reckon that's the sexiest and most expensive jockstrap ever," he remarked. "Do all the studs have diamonds under them?"

"No there are only twenty diamonds."

"Only! Right the next thing I need to know is who the contact is."

Jim and Wellington looked at each other, and then Wellington spilled the beans.

"He's a guy by the name of Vlasek."

"Not Vlasek Kalkavic?" asked Heinz.

Wellington nodded.

"We've been after him for years. He's a smuggler of renown."

"Heinz, I've got one question I want answered," I appealed.

"What's the problem, Mike?"

"Is it possible that nothing will be done to either Jim or Wellington and that they'll be able to leave the country without any complications or court cases?"

Heinz gave both Wellington and Jim a cold stare, possibly to make them feel embarrassed, then added, "we'll have to see if they co-operate with me. Will you?"

After much hesitation, both men agreed to co-operate with Heinz.

"This is what you're going to do," said Heinz and he began to explain the plan.

Once Heinz had finished explaining what was expected of the two men and how the plan would work, we all went back to the bar and had drinks. For the rest of the night, Jim and Wellington remained somewhat subdued and when we returned to the hotel, they didn't say much to each other or to Chad or me.

14

CONATCT IS MADE

The whole of the following day everyone seemed subdued and tense,. At breakfast, Chad and I spoke but Jim and Wellington remained pretty quiet. In my heart I felt that Jim was angry with me, but I wasn't going to let it get me down; I had Chad and an uncle who was alive and well, at least at the moment. Nothing much was planned for the day, in fact, both men remained at the hotel all day. Chad and I went shopping and tried to relax as much as we could, but as the hands of the clocks neared 6:00p.m, we became more anxious.

"I hope everything goes well for them, Chad."

"I'm sure it will, provided they do exactly what Heinz has told them to do."

"I'm glad that Heinz promised that nothing would be done to Jim or Wellington. I think that knowing that, has taken a load off my shoulders because I was worried that we'd be going home while they rotted in a German jail."

"Talking about going back, what do you think they're going to do after all this is over?" asked Chad.

"Haven't a clue but I'm assuming we'll be going back soon as they will have got rid of the diamonds and it might put a damper on the whole holiday. But what about you?"

"What do you mean?"

"Well when we go back are you going home and will I see you again?"

Chad stared in horror at me.

"I'm heading back to Toronto and I'm spending Christmas with my folks, then I'm going to ... where is it you live?"

"Fort Lauderdale!"

"Oh yes, that beach resort. Well I thought I'd go to Fort Lauderdale to spend New Years with my boyfriend and his family; that is if they want me!"

"You're likely to be put over my knee and given a hiding if you talk like that."

"If it means getting a spanking from you, then I'll continue to talk like that," answered Chad.

"I'd love you to meet my folks," I said, hugging Chad and kissing his sweet lips. "And then what happens after that?"

"We'll have to discuss that, but I don't believe in living apart," replied Chad.

"I'm very glad to hear that because I couldn't live without you."

I looked at my wristwatch and told Chad we had better get moving, so we headed down to the river where we saw Wellington and Jim waiting to board the cruise boat which would take its passengers along the Rhine River to view the evening lights. I had previously removed the diamonds from under the studs in my jockstrap and Jim had placed them in the velvet bag that he carried with him. Heinz had already positioned himself aboard the *S.S. Rheingold,* along with two members of the Cologne police force, while on the land waited two more plain-clothes detectives should the contact try to escape from the boat once it docked. Although Heinz had told Chad and I to wait on shore, I was eager to get on board to safeguard Wellington and Jim. Henk had also come to join us because the club wouldn't open till later. Finally at five minutes to six, Jim and Wellington boarded the boat and at six precisely, she set sail for her voyage along the Rhine River.

Jim and Wellington found themselves two seats near the rear of the boat and sat down. Heinz and his colleagues sat nearby and waited for the contact to arrive. Wellington had been able to describe himself to the contact and being the only Black guy on board the boat, it wouldn't be difficult for the contact to pick him out.

Chad and I stood on the banks of the Rhine, watching the *Rheingold* move up river. We could see both our friends at the rear and I also spotted Heinz. The boat eventually grew smaller to us and we could do nothing but wait.

On board a person allocated the job, began to give a commentary as he boat sailed past various tourist sights and the passengers either sat or stood against the railings and watched the passing shoreline.

A dark haired, thin man of about five foot ten approached the rear of the boat and leaned over the side to watch the wake that the boat had created. He looked to be about forty years of age, had a short goatee and dark, brooding eyes. Jim and Wellington noticed him but did nothing. After five minutes the man approached the only empty seat next to Wellington and sat down.

"It is a lovely evening," he said with a thick foreign accent.

"Yes, it is," replied Wellington.

After that nothing more was said.

The boat continued its journey and then turned to head back to its starting point. Nothing had taken place, but everyone kept their places. When the boat was about a kilometer from the docking area, the dark haired man spoke again.

"You have something for me?"

"Only if you have something for me," answered Wellington.

The man tapped the breast pocket of the jacket he was wearing. Neither Jim nor Wellington were aware if he had a weapon of any sort on him, so by tapping his pocket could have meant he had a gun hidden there, or it might have been the cash.

"Let me see the goods," requested the man.

Jim handed over the velvet bag containing the diamonds to Wellington, who opened the bag and took out a diamond which he held in the palm of his hand so other passengers could not see. The man took the diamond from Wellington and looked at it. Then he held it up to the sky as if to look through it, but in doing this, he pretended that he was shielding his eyes in some way. He then returned the diamond to Wellington's palm.

"How many?"

"As I promised, twenty," said Wellington, opening the velvet bag and showing the man.

"One hundred thousand Euros as promised?" said the man.

"Correct," replied Wellington.

As the man put his hand into his jacket breast pocket, Jim and Wellington tensed, so did Heinz and his men, but a thick envelope appeared and the man handed it to Wellington who opened it and checked its contents. Satisfied, Wellington handed over the velvet bag and the man immediately rose from his seat, after checking his contents and headed to the front of the boat. Jim and Wellington sighed with relief and quickly Heinz and his men rose and followed their suspect, Vlasek Kalkavic. Wellington handed Jim the envelope and the two men smiled briefly to each other.

Meanwhile as the boat neared its mooring, Heinz and his two officers closed in on either side of Vlasek.

"Mr. Vlasek Kalkavic, you are under arrest for being in possession of stolen goods, will you please come with us," said Heinz very formally and forcefully.

They handcuffed Vlasek and waited for the boat to tie up, and as soon as that had been done, they frog-marched him off the boat and into a waiting car. Jim and Wellington casually walked down the gangplank where they were met by Chad, Henk and me.

"Did you enjoy the trip and the views?" I asked as we walked casually away from the boat.

I could see that Jim was sweating profusely.

"Have they taken him away?" asked the nervous Jim.

"Yes, so would you like to go for a drink now?" asked Chad.

"What a ridiculous question" I need more than one drink," retorted Jim.

The guys left to go to the nearest bar while Heinz and his men drove Vlasek to the central police station where he was formally charged and imprisoned.

15

GRATITUDE

At 9:30 that evening, after Chad Wellington, Jim and I had feasted but not touched the money in the envelope; we made our way to the club where we had promised to meet up with Henk and Heinz. Both brothers were there waiting for us when we arrived, and both had donned their best leathers to make our evening.

The first thing that Jim did when he saw Heinz was to buy him a drink.

"I want to say a special thanks you to you Heinz for getting us out of this predicament, but I must add, it couldn't have happened if it weren't for Mike and Chad who, I must admit, angered me by calling you, Heinz, but once I realized their genuine concern was for my and Wellington's safety, I then appreciated what they were trying to do. Henk I have to thank you for contacting Heinz and getting the most decent cop in Germany to help us. Finally, Wellington, I'm sorry to have landed you in so much trouble; it was not my intention. And so I would like to make a toast to you guys who are so special to me. Thank you for everything."

"Cheers," we all shouted.

Heinz then stood up and towered over us on our bar stools.

"First tell me how you felt while on the boat, Jim?"

"Nervous, especially thinking that he might have had a gun on him; anxious for Wellington's safety because he was the one who had to do all the talking and then worrying that he might get away from your guys, Heinz."

"You had nothing to fear because as I told you when we did the planning, there would be other police on the boat as well as on the land, surveying our every move. And you, Wellington, what were you feeling?"

"I was shitting myself!"

We all roared with laughter at Wellington's expression of honesty.

"So what was the outcome, Heinz?" asked Jim.

"What's happened was that we laid a charge against him of being in possession of illicit diamonds. As far as we were concerned there was no money that changed hands and he had boarded the boat already with the diamonds in his possession."

"So there won't be any charges against us and no court case for us?" asked Jim.

"It's what I promised you. The money that you acquired you can do what you like with it."

Jim looked at Wellington and he returned the look.

"I would very much like to give both you and Henk something, Heinz; for your willingness to help us, but I need some help here. Earlier when we met Henk, he told us he was the naughty son, so whatever money I give you, I don't want you buying anything that might be construed as being naughty. Understand?"

"Yes Dad," said Henk jokingly.

"If I can make a suggestion," said Heinz, "my share I would like you to give to a charity of my choice and Henk's share, put into trust so he can't touch it."

"Are you serious?" enquired Jim.

Heinz laughed.

"I'm serious about mine, but you can give Henk his. If he wants to spend it on drugs, which I hope he won't, that's his decision."

"Mike and Chad, I would like to give you boys something as well, if I may."

"Jim, we don't want anything from you. You have given us this whole holiday and the excitement that came with it, so we don't need anything else, but thank you all the same."

"Are you speaking for yourself, Mike?"

"No, Jim, I'm speaking for both of us."

"Well if that's the way you feel, when you two decide to settle together, and decide to cement your relationship, then you're coming to London for your honeymoon."

"OK that's a deal," I replied.

"What about you, Chad?"

"Whatever Mike wants, I'll go along with that."

"You see that's what a typical partner would say. It's as if they've been together for years already," quipped Jim.

"Well, we're hoping to be together for years," I retorted. "Can I buy anyone another drink?"

Chad and Heinz asked for another, but Jim said he was still busy and Henk was busy attending to customers.

"Heinz, if you ever come over to London, you have to contact Wellington and me and come and stay with us," said Jim, "and that goes for Henk as well. Of course you can both come together."

"We often do," relied Heinz with a wry grin on his face.

"I'm sure you do, and you can do that as well," said Jim. "Henk has told us how he enjoys having sex with his brother and I think it's brilliant that you two have such a close bond together."

Heinz laughed at Jim's comment about him and Henk have sex.

"You know, I've never said this to anyone, let alone Henk, but if I was to go into a relationship with anyone, it would be with someone like Henk. The other reason I enjoy having sex with him is because we understand each other so well and we know what the other one likes and doesn't like so when we're in bed or in the club here together and we're making out, he knows what triggers my cock and I know what sends his into orbit. I don't know if you know, but I think he's also got the tightest ass I've ever been in."

"Really!" said all of us together.

Heinz realized what he'd said then added, "Oh dear, I'm giving trade secrets away, aren't I."

"Not at all," replied Jim. "It's always good to know these sorts of things, isn't it boys?"

"Absolutely," chorused the rest of us.

"And I know exactly what you're talking about with regards to that tight ass of his…," said Wellington, with a satisfied smile on his face.

"Have you had a taste of it, Wellington?" asked Heinz.

"Oh yes!"

Chad and I decided to take ourselves onto the dance floor for a while, leaving Wellington and Jim with Heinz..

"Heinz, when are you going back to Berlin?" asked Jim.

"Tomorrow. I just have to complete the paper work and then I can get home."

"I was wondering, and I'm sure Wellington was also, but would you and Henk like to come round to our hotel after he goes off duty for a nightcap with Wellington and me?"

"That sounds like a great idea and I know Henk would like that too," replied Heinz, let's ask him. Henk!'"

Henk came over to Heinz.

"Wellington and Jim have invited us to go back to their place after you close up for a drink with them. Would you like to go?"

"Very much, thanks, but I don't have to close up tonight, so we can go whenever you guys want to."

"Why, who's closing up?"

"Fritz is and he's here already, so I can leave now if I like."

Heinz and Henk looked at Wellington and Jim and all four faces lit up.

"Well then let's go," said Jim. I'll just tell Mike that we're going."

Jim came onto the dance floor and told Chad and me that they were going so I knew what was planned between them.

"No problem, I shouted over the blasting music. "We'll see you in the morning. Enjoy the night, you horny man," I added, giving Jim a wink.

Jim, Wellington, Henk and Heinz, left the club and made their way back to the hotel, where they ordered a couple of drinks and made their way up to Jim and Wellington's bedroom.

"What do you actually do, Jim?" enquired Heinz.

"I suppose you could call me a financier."

"And this diamond business, is it a regular thing?"

Jim laughed.

"Not at all. This was something that Wellington and I tried for the first time."

"And I hope the last time," echoed Heinz.

The drinks flowed and it wasn't long before Henk was feeling Wellington's muscular legs and his hands were wandering higher until they reached the magical large package. When Jim and Heinz noticed this they began to get busty together and soon all four were all over each other. Partners were being swapped and Jim and Wellington were fascinated when Henk and Heinz started sucking each other's cocks. The passions were building and soon arms, legs, mouths, asses and cocks were being attacked.

In the early hours of the morning, Henk and Heinz slipped out of the bedroom, both satisfied and replete and left. In the other room, Chad and I slept arms wrapped around each other's warm body, our cocks hard as we dreamed of our future together.

16

ALL GOOD THINGS COME TO AN END.

Chad was the first to wake up and went into the bathroom. I heard the toilet flush and then he returned to our bed.

"Morning, beautiful," he said, leaning over me and kissing me gently on the lips. "Did you sleep well?"

"Hm, yes except for that big, hard cock that kept prodding me all night," I answered, yawning.

"And what about the one that constantly prodded me all night. I'm surprised my ass is still in one piece."

"You wish I had split your ass, don't you?"

"So why didn't you? You had every opportunity last night, so if you didn't, that's your loss, sexy."

"I wonder how Jim and Wellington went last night," I mused. "I can only imagine what fun there would have been in that room; four hot guys all at each other."

"Do you think that Henk and Heinz will still be there this morning?"

"I know Heinz said he had to get back to Berlin this morning, so maybe they left last night or in the early hours this morning," I answered.

"Mike I think I'm going to have to book my return flight today."

"Do you have to leave so soon, Chad?"

"I've got to get back to work, but it doesn't mean that I'm not going to see you. Remember I told you I was coming to spend New Year with you and meet your family."

"I can't wait for that and then we can discuss my coming to Toronto with you."

"Would you be willing to live in Toronto with me?"

"I'd live anywhere with you. But seriously, you're already settled there with a job and I don't have one yet, so it makes sense for me to come and live with you in Toronto rather than you coming to live in Fort Lauderdale, don't you agree?"

"I'd be honored to have you moving to Toronto, but we could always go to Fort Lauderdale for our holidays, couldn't we?"

"Absolutely."

"I'll ask at reception where the nearest travel agency is so that I can book my flight and if you've got nothing planned for today, maybe we could get the booking out of the way and then spend time together, just the two of us."

"I'd like that. Jim and Wellington can go out for the day if necessary."

"Come on, let's have a shower together," suggested Chad.

Chad and I went into the bathroom, turned on the shower and stood under the spray of warm water and caressed each other's body bringing each other to a full arousal. Half an hour later, two clean, loving and well-satisfied young men emerged from the bathroom.

At breakfast, Jim and Wellington glowed. In fact all four were glowing happily. I told Jim that Chad was going to book his return flight that day and so Jim thought it a good idea to book ours at the same time, so after we had finished our breakfast, we set off to find the travel agency that the receptionist and told us about.

At the agency, Chad was booked on a flight leaving that night, direct to New York and then on to Toronto; while we booked on a flight to London the same time Chad would be leaving, and then I would leave for Fort Lauderdale the day after we had arrived in London. I felt sad that our holiday was coming to an end, but I was happy with the outcome of our holiday, especially having met Chad.

"I don't know what you guys are going to do today," I said to Jim and Wellington, "but Chad and I want some time to ourselves, if you don't mind."

"Of course you should spend time together. I think we'll probably pack our bags and notify the hotel that we'll be leaving. I think Wellington might see if he can see Henk, but I won't be doing anything gout of the usual," said Jim.

We left the travel agency and went back to the hotel where Chad and I put the 'Do Not Disturb' sign on the bedroom door and then collapsed onto our bed to make love for the rest of the day.

Early in the afternoon, we all made our way to the airport to catch our various flights. When I watched Chad disappear through the gate to board his flight, tears welled up in my eyes, but Jim and Wellington were there to comfort me.

Then it was our turn to board our flight to London. We boarded our aircraft and found our seats. The funny thing was that there was not the same excitement we had when we left for Amsterdam, but I think both Wellington and Jim were pleased to be going home.

I sat next to the window with Wellington next to me, and after we had taken off, I asked him whether Henk and Heinz had stayed the whole night with them.

"They left in the early hours of the morning," he replied.

"And did you manage to see him before we flew today?"

"I popped round to the club and fortunately he was there so we spent some time together and told him he had to come and visit us in London."

"And last night,; was it fun with the four of you together?"

"Oh yes," said Wellington with delight.

"So tell me more. Give me all the juicy details. Did the brothers make out with each other?" I begged.

"That's a whole story on its own, Mike."

"So tell it to me. I like to hear the juicy details."

"Suffer baby, suffer! Maybe another time I'll fill you in on the details, now get some rest and go to sleep."

I didn't like to be rebuffed but I knew that sooner or later I would get all the details of their horny night together.

During the flight, we placed blankets over our legs to stay warm and tried to doze. As I lay in my seat, I felt Wellington's hand rest on my crotch and then start to rub over my cock in an effort to get it hard. It didn't take long for that to happen and when he felt I was hard enough, he leaned over lifted my blanket, buried his head under it, unzipped my jeans, pulled out my erection and began to slurp on my thick cock until I shot my load down his throat. I tried to keep as quiet as possible when I came and when he had drained me of all my juice, he pulled his head from under the blanket, squeezed my thigh and said, "Welcome to the mile high club, honey, elementary level."

"Elementary?" I questioned, quietly.

"Yes, a blowjob is worth an elementary level; a full fuck is to achieve the full mile high club status."

"Thanks Wellington, That was delicious."

I turned to face Jim and noticed he was smiling but with his eyes closed. I wasn't sure whether he had watched Wellington's actions of he was asleep and dreaming.

When we arrived back at Heathrow Airport, we caught the express to Paddington Station and then got a cab to Chelsea. The moment that we entered Jim's apartment, Wellington resumed his role of manservant and all informality disappeared. I became Master Michael once more and Jim was Master James and even his formal speech returned. It was like I'd been in a dream-like state and had returned to normality, hearing what could be considered 'posh' English being spoken.

After spending a wonderful day with Jim and Wellington in London and enjoying a meal prepared by Wellington, I fell into bed and dreamed of Chad and rose early the following morning to head back to Heathrow to catch my flight back to the States.

Although I was sitting alone on my flight, it gave me time to contemplate my holiday. I was immensely pleased at meeting Chad and I was so proud of myself that I had saved Wellington and Jim from their own greed and possible incarceration, but above all I was grateful for the holiday as it made me grow up quickly, not that I hadn't, but I came back with a more mature outlook and some very nice new friends.

As for what happened on my last night in London…well that's another story which I'll tell you one day, and I'm sure if you ask Wellington, he's not going to tell either.

ABOUT THE AUTHOR

Lew Bull

LEW BULL recently had his fifth novel published, entitled *Shadows*. This novel adds to his collection of mystery stories titled, *Power Buddies; Wet, Wild & Willing; The Bonds of Friendship* and *Caribbean Cruising*. Added to these are his recently published two anthologies, one of exotic cocktail recipes accompanied by equally erotic stories entitled, *Cocktales* and the other, *Mystique*. His novel *Wet, Wild & Willing* was nominated for the 2008 National Leather Association (International) writing award. Other recent anthologies that contain his work include, *Cruise Lines; Taken By Force; Boys Will Be Boys; Don't Ask, Don't Tie Me Up - Military BDSM Fantasies; Service with a Smile; Pretty Boys & Roughnecks; Special Forces* and *Sex Time-Travel*. He is still involved in education and lives in Johannesburg, South Africa where he enjoys spending time with his partner of thirty-two years and traveling as often as he can.

Bull

POWER BUDDIES

Power
Buddies

a novel by
LEW BULL

A
BONER
BOOK

A NOVEL BY

Lew Bull

Wet, Wild

and Willing

The sexcapades of a single man

(spine) Bull

(spine) WET, WILD AND WILLING

A BONER BOOK

tales

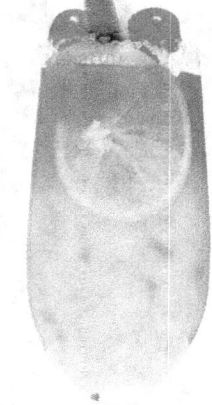

by

Lew Bull

Bull

Caribbean Cruising

Caribbean Cruising

a novel by
Lew Bull

A
Boner
Book

The Bonds of Friendship

Friendship

Lew Bull

A
Boner
Book

(spine) Bull

(spine) The Bonds of Friendship

MYSTIQUE

LEW
BULL

BULL

MYSTIQUE

A
BONER
BOOK

MEMOIRS OF A
HUSTLER

MEMOIRS OF A HUSTLER

BULL

A NOVEL BY
LEW BULL

A
BONER
BOOK